All the World's a Stage

Volume III

by Joann Leonard

SAMUELFRENCH.COM

No one shall commit or authorize any act or omission by which the copyright of, or the right to copyright, this play may be impaired.

No one shall make any changes in this play for the purpose of production.

Publication of this play does not imply availability for performance. Both amateurs and professionals considering a production are strongly advised in their own interests to apply to Samuel French, Inc., for written permission before starting rehearsals, advertising, or booking a theatre.

No part of this book may be reproduced, stored in a retrieval system, or transmitted in any form, by any means, now known or yet to be invented, including mechanical, electronic, photocopying, recording, videotaping, or otherwise, without the prior written permission of the publisher.

MUSIC USE NOTE

Licensees are solely responsible for obtaining formal written permission from copyright owners to use copyrighted music in the performance of this play and are strongly cautioned to do so. If no such permission is obtained by the licensee, then the licensee must use only original music that the licensee owns and controls. Licensees are solely responsible and liable for all music clearances and shall indemnify the copyright owners of the play and their licensing agent, Baker's Plays, against any costs, expenses, losses and liabilities arising from the use of music by licensees.

IMPORTANT BILLING AND CREDIT
REQUIREMENTS

All producers of *ALL THE WORLD'S A STAGE, VOLUME III must* give credit to the Author of the Play in all programs distributed in connection with performances of the Play, and in all instances in which the title of the Play appears for the purposes of advertising, publicizing or otherwise exploiting the Play and/or a production. The name of the Author *must* appear on a separate line on which no other name appears, immediately following the title and *must* appear in size of type not less than fifty percent of the size of the title type. Also, the following notice must appear on all printed programs, "Produced by special arrangement with Baker's Plays."

CONTENTS

THE HEALING LEAVES

A folktale from Russia

The Healing Leaves was first presented by Metastages Theatre Centre on April 25, 1998 at the Paul Robeson Cultural Center, Penn State University, University Park, Pennsylvania. The cultural resource advisors were Tatiana Bibikova, Dr. Lorraine Kapitanoff, and Fedor & Yuri Sarhin. The production was directed by the author and included the following cast:

STORYTELLER 1 . . . . Sara Fitzwater

STORYTELLER 2 . . . . .Matt Drosnes

CZAR/DRAGON . . . . George Feasler

CZARINA/SNAKE . . . . .Alicia Albright

IRINA/SNAKE . . . . .Eszter Gordon

VLADIMIR . . . . .Daniel Thompson

OLGA . . . . .Emily Weiner

IGOR . . . . .Billy Mulberger

LARISSA/PATH OF NO RETURN . . . . Francis Otano-Gracia

ADVISOR/A HAPPY JOURNEY . . . . Nahir Otano-Gracia

PHYSICIAN/SERPENT . . . . Toby Squier-Roper

INNKEEPER/SNAKE . . . . Kristine Crassweller

ALEXI . . . . Charles Lumpkins

BABA YAGA 1 . . . . .Emily Weiner

BABA YAGA 2 . . . . .Melissa Peragine

QUEEN OF NO RETURN . . . . Erin Calandra

CHARACTERS

STORYTELLER 1
STORYTELLER 2
CZAR
CZARINA
IRINA
OLGA
LARISSA
PRINCE VLADIMIR
PRINCE IGOR
ALEXI, THE PAUPER
PHYSICIAN
INNKEEPER
BABA YAGA 1
BABA YAGA 2
ADVISOR
DRAGON
VIPER
QUEEN OF NO RETURN

STORYTELLER 1. To all children in the three and seventh, three eleventh kingdom.

STORYTELLER 2. That's how Russian stories always begin.

STORYTELLER 1. And it begins here on top of a cozy Russian stove, a brick and clay box with a gentle fire glowing inside, a stove big enough not only to bake in –

STORYTELLER 2. and to cook on –

STORYTELLER 1. but also to sleep on during the bitter cold nights.

STORYTELLER 2. And it is on top of a Russian stove where the storyteller sits and tells stories that will warm you right down to the bottom of your…

STORYTELLER 1. …your heart.

STORYTELLER 2. Right. This is the story of the healing leaves. It begins with a problem that frequently happened long ago.

STORYTELLER 1. Maybe you have heard of it. It's the situation that arises when parents have a definite plan for their children –

STORYTELLER 2. And their children also have a definite plan.

BOTH. A different one!

STORYTELLER 1. So. To all children in the three and seventh, three eleventh kingdom, once there lived a Czar and Czarina who had three lovely daughters.

*(Enter **CZAR** and **CZARINA** and **THREE DAUGHTERS**.)*

CZAR. So my daughters, remember. When you marry, you are to choose only princes who are….

CZARINA. Wealthy.

CZAR. Yes. Very wealthy. Stables of fine horses, castles, servants…

DAUGHTERS. Yes, Papa.

CZARINA. And of course a treasury full of gold, jewels, and silver goblets.

DAUGHTERS. Yes, Mama.

CZARINA. And handsome.

CZAR. Noble lineage, muscular, Mother Russia's finest sons...

DAUGHTERS. Yes, Papa.

CZARINA. Go now and choose well.

DAUGHTERS. Yes, Mama.

   (**DAUGHTERS** *exit.*)

STORYTELLER 2. And so it was that the daughters were married. Irina, the first daughter, married Vladimir, a very handsome and very wealthy prince.

   (**IRINA** *enters with* **VLADIMIR.**)

CZARINA. A good match. Our Irina wants for nothing.

IRINA. It's true. Every morning, on my silver breakfast tray, I find a new ring.

VLADIMIR. Or a bracelet.

IRINA. *(laughing)* Yes. Or a bracelet.

CZAR. And Olga.

   (*Enter* **OLGA** *and* **IGOR.**)

   Her husband, Prince Igor, lavishes her with the finest of everything.

OLGA. Every evening, our supper of roasted pheasant, stroganoff and venison in burgundy sauce is served on golden dishes.

IGOR. Engraved with our initials.

OLGA. "O."

IGOR. "I."

STORYTELLERS. *(looking at each other)* Oi ?

ADVISOR. Supper is served, Your Majesties.

CZARINA. Splendid. Let us go in. There is a sumptuous repast waiting.

IRINA. But what about Larissa and her husband Alexi, the peasant?

OLGA. They are not here yet.

CZAR. Nor will they be. Ever!

CZARINA. Your father has forbidden them to set foot in the palace.

IRINA. But they love each other.

CZAR. I forbade them to get married and she disobeyed.

OLGA. Alexi may be poor, but at least he and Larissa are happy.

IRINA. Yet, when I am riding in my coach to the dressmakers, I see our poor sister hanging out laundry and digging potatoes outside their hut.

OLGA. Poor Larissa, princess of a potato patch. Unimaginable!

CZAR. Precisely. That's what comes from ignoring your father.

CZARINA. There you go, getting yourself hotter than a steaming samovar. Calm yourself, dear. Supper is waiting, children.

(**PRINCES** *and* **PRINCESSES** *exit.*)

STORYTELLER 1. Some weeks later the king awoke one morning and though his eyes were wide open, he could not see.

ADVISOR. Sit here, sire. The physician from Gorki should be arriving soon.

CZAR. What difference does it make. Physicians have come from Minsk, Leningrad, Karkov and I'm still blind as a mole at midnight.

CZARINA. We must not despair. Perhaps this time…

ADVISOR. Here is the physician.

PHYSICIAN. *(bowing)* Zdravstvuyte your majesties. *(examines the* **CZAR***'s eyes)* Do your eyes burn, Sire?

CZAR. No.

PHYSICIAN. Do they itch?

CZAR. No!

PHYSICIAN. Do they water or crust?

CZAR. No!!!

PHYSICIAN. *(takes out a silver coin and flashes it in front of the* **CZAR***'s eyes)* Can you see a flicker, a flash?

CZAR. Nothing.

PHYSICIAN. Then, there is only one cure for your blind-ness.

CZARINA. A cure!

CZAR. What is it?

PHYSICIAN. Far away in the Land of No Return there is a tree whose leaves can heal blindness.

ADVISOR. I will dispatch someone immediately. *(starts to go)*

PHYSICIAN. You should know, sire, that no one who has attempted to find these leaves has ever returned. That is why it is called the Land of No Return.

CZAR. What choice do I have? Advisor, summon my sons-in law, Prince Vladimir and Prince Igor.

ADVISOR. As you wish, Sire.

    *(**ADVISOR** leaves.)*

PHYSICIAN. *(bows)* I wish you good fortune in your search. By your leave, majesty.

    *(**PHYSICIAN** exits. **ADVISOR** re-enters with **PRINCE IGOR** and **PRINCE VLADIMIR**.)*

STORYTELLER 2. When Prince Vladimir and Prince Igor arrived, the Czar told them about the wonderful heal-ing leaves.

VLAD/IGOR. Your Majesty.

CZAR. If you come back with the leaves, I will give each of you one third of my kingdom.

VLADIMIR. You are more than generous, Sire.

CZAR. Yes. But, if you return without the leaves, I will have you banished.

ALL. What?

IGOR. *(looking at* **VLADIMIR***)* Banished?

CZARINA. Oh dear, I'm sure you don't mean banished.

CZAR. Banished! Dire consequences promote increased effort.

CZARINA. But such harsh punishment!

CZAR. I may lack sight, but I have insight into how the world works. Go now.

CZARINA. Do svidaniya, my brave sons.. A safe and speedy return.

> *(***PRINCES** *exit.)*

Come, dear. You should rest now.

CZAR. Yes, yes. That's all I do is rest.

> *(***ADVISOR** *helps* **CZAR** *off.* **LARISSA** *sees that the coast is clear and sneaks in to see her mother.)*

LARISSA. *(whispering)* Mother, Mother…

CZARINA. Larissa?

LARISSA. Are you alone?

CZARINA. Yes, yes. Oh my dear child. *(embraces her)* How deeply I've missed you. Here, let me look at you. Are you all right?

LARISSA. I'm fine. I came because I heard about Father's blindness.

CZARINA. My dear, dear Larissa.

LARISSA. I know that you and Father turned me out because my husband, Alexi, is a peasant. But Mother, he is a good man, strong of heart and with a pure soul. I know that if anyone can return with the healing leaves to restore Father's sight, it is Alexi.

CZARINA. But do you understand the conditions? If he fails, he will be banished and you will never see each other again.

LARISSA. Yes, Alexi understands and accepts the conditions.

CZARINA. Very well. Let us go and ask the cook for some provisions for his journey.

LARISSA. Thank you, Mother. For Father's sake, I pray he will succeed, and for my sake, that he returns home safely.

CZARINA. I pray the same.

(They exit.)

STORYTELLER 1. Meanwhile Prince Vladimir and Prince Igor, inquiring about the way to the Land of No Return, made a terrifying discovery about the road that led to the healing leaves.

*(***PRINCES*** enter.)*

VLADIMIR. A dragon?

IGOR. And a viper?

VLADIMIR. They will destroy anyone who comes near?

IGOR. No way!

VLADIMIR. Look, an inn. Let's stay here until we decide what to do.

IGOR. We either stay here, or go back home without the leaves to banishment.

VLADIMIR. At least we are princes and have plenty of money. We can eat, drink and live in comfort. It could be worse.

INNKEEPER. Zdravstvuite. Welcome, gentlemen. Come and sit by the fire.

PRINCES. Thank you, innkeeper.

STORYTELLER 2. Two weeks later, the peasant Alexi arrived at the inn. He recognized Prince Vladimir and Prince Igor, but they did not notice him.

ALEXI. Zdravstvuite. Good day.

INNKEEPER. Zdravstvuite.

ALEXI. I am searching for the healing leaves that can be found in the Land of No Return.

*(***VLADIMIR*** and ***IGOR*** look up.)*

INNKEEPER. The road to the Land of No Return is perilous, friend. A viper and a dragon guard the road and destroy anyone who approaches. No one has ever returned.

ALEXI. Do you know how to get there?

INNKEEPER. No, nyet, nyet.

ALEXI. Does anyone know the way?

INNKEEPER. Do you have onions for ears? Even if you get there, you'll never return.

ALEXI. So no one knows how to get there?

INNKEEPER. Yes, my pigheaded fellow. There are some creatures who know how to gain entry.

ALEXI. Who are they?

INNKEEPER. Why, the Baba Yagas who live in the valley. Only one problem.

ALEXI. What is that?

INNKEEPER. One Baba Yaga kills anyone who comes within reach. I'm sure she would use your bones to pick her teeth.

(*Laughs heartily.* **PRINCES** *laugh.*)

ALEXI. We'll see. Thank you for your help. (*starts to leave*)

VLADIMIR. You're not intending to visit the Baba Yagas, are you?

ALEXI. Da. (*nodding head yes*)

IGOR. You must have a fool's brains.

INNKEEPER. But not for long.

(**PRINCES** *and* **INNKEEPER** *laugh and exit.*)

ALEXI. Do svidaniya.

STORYTELLER 1. Alexi, though poor, did not lack for courage. Unafraid, he set out for the valley, searching until he found the hut of the Baba Yagas.

STORYTELLER 2. The friendly Baba Yaga saw him approach and rushed to warn him.

BABA 1. (*runs to him*) Stop where you are.

ALEXI. Zdrastvuite. Hello.

BABA 1. You must leave immediately. My sister is a cranky Baba Yaga. If she finds you here she will kill you.

ALEXI. I must speak with her. I need directions to the Land of No Return.

BABA 1. You've got more nerve than a herring has bones! Don't say I didn't warn you. Here she comes now. Quickly, hide.

BABA 2. *(enters)* Meat! Blood! Human smell!

BABA 1. Your nose must be playing tricks on you. Blow it.

(**BABA 2** *starts to use sleeve.*)

And don't be using your sleeve. Here. *(hands her a rag)*

BABA 2. *(blows noisily and sniffs air)* Human meat. I know it when I smell it. Where is my knife?

ALEXI. *(popping out)* What a fine nose you have to smell something as puny as me.

BABA 2. *(taken aback)* What?

ALEXI. You are my host and may do with me as you wish, but if you would allow me to tell you a story first.

BABA 2. Puny thing to have so much courage.

BABA 1. More metal than an iron cauldron.

BABA 2. Haven't heard a story in a long while. Go ahead.

STORYTELLER 1. So Alexi told the Baba Yagas about the Czar's blindness and about having to go to the Land of No Return to find the healing leaves.

BABA 2. First man I've met who wasn't a lily-livered, chicken-shuffling, son-of-a-termite. Because you are not afraid of me or the Land of No Return, I will not kill you. Do this. Walk seven days. Come to the fork in the road. One road has a sign that reads "A Happy Journey," the other road has a sign that reads "He who follows this path shall not return." That is the road you take. Next you will come to a valley filled with huge brown snakes...

BABA 1. Black, they are black snakes.

BABA 2. Brown, black. What difference. No man has ever passed through it . When you come to the snakes you must say... *(thinks)* you must say....

BABA 1. What a beautiful valley filled with honey.

BABA 2. That's right. The snakes will disappear. Next you will come to a palace guarded by a dragon and viper. If they appear to be sleeping, they are awake. If they look awake, they are sleeping.

BABA 1. Wait until they are asleep.

BABA 2. Then go into the queen's chamber. Beside her bed is a tree with the healing leaves. Fill a bag with the leaves...

BABA 1. And be sure to stuff as many as you can in your pockets.

BABA 2. Then, take the Queen's ring off her finger and put it on your finger. Then go.

BABA 1. And on the way back do everything you did before, only backwards. Queen.

BABA 1. Viper.

BABA 2. Dragon.

BABA 1. Awake, sleeping.

BABA 2. Sleeping, awake.

BABA 1. Snakes.

BABA 2. "Beautiful valley filled with honey."

BABA 1. Fork in the road.

BABA 2. Follow the path of no return.

BABA 1. Walk seven days.

ALEXI. I will! Thank you both. I will do as you have told me.

BABA YAGAS: Good luck.

    (**BABA YAGAS** *exit.*)

STORYTELLER 2. Alexi followed the Baba Yagas instructions and eventually reached the palace.

    (*Mime accompanied by music of journey to the fork in the road, snake-filled valley, palace with dragon and viper. Actors will portray everything on the journey – the signposts, snakes, viper and dragon.*)

There Alexi waited.

ALEXI. Asleep means awake. Awake means asleep.

(Monsters awake.)

I must hurry.

STORYTELLER 1. Alexi tiptoed in, *(goes and gets leaves and takes ring off* **QUEEN***)* silently filled his bag and his pockets with leaves, gently slipped the ring from the Queen's finger and put it on his own, and left the Land of No Return and came, once again, to the inn.

(Mime of return to music — all the mime and motions in reverse.)

INNKEEPER. Zdravstvuite, hello. Our tattered fellow returns alive!

VLADIMIR. *(suspiciously)* He is a bag of bones, but his sack is fat.

IGOR. What do you have in your sack, good fellow.

ALEXI. Leaves. Healing leaves!

*(***PRINCES*** look astonished.)*

VLADIMIR. Healing leaves. Interesting. Innkeeper, bring a cup of warm brew for this fellow. He's had a trying journey. *(quietly aside)* And, Igor, the elixir.

IGOR. What elixir?

VLADIMIR. You know. *(fraught with subtext)* The elixir for *weary* people.

IGOR. Oh. Ha, ha. *That* elixir. Of course. Of course. *(removes a small vial from his person)* Try some of this in your brew, friend. It will make you feel very…uh…

VLADIMIR. Very "re-leaved."

IGOR. Relieved. Yes. Relieved of your lee….

*(***VLADIMIR*** elbows **IGOR**.)*

VLADIMIR. Put your bag down and come rest.

*(***VLADIMIR*** takes cup from **INNKEEPER** and hands it to **IGOR** who pours in the elixir. **IGOR** hands cup to **ALEXI**. They raise cups.)*

PRINCES. Nah zdoroviya, to your health.

ALEXI. Nah zdoroviya. And to yours.

(They drink. **ALEXI** *falls asleep.)*

VLADIMIR. Take these.

*(***VLADIMIR** *hands drinks to* **INNKEEPER,** *who exits.)*

Now rub some of the elixir in his eyes to blind him. Grab that bag of healing leaves.

IGOR. It will certainly heal the condition that ails *us*, ha, ha, ha.

(They both laugh.)

VLADIMIR. Let's drag this millstone outside and throw him in the ditch by the road.

(They do so.)

STORYTELLER 2. Once they had disposed of Alexi in the ditch, Prince Vladimir and Prince Igor hurried back to the palace.

(Enter **DAUGHTERS** *to greet them.)*

They were given a heroes' welcome.

(Enter **ADVISOR, CZAR, CZARINA.***)*

CZARINA. Our prayers are answered. You have returned safely from the Land of No Return.

IGOR. Try these, Father.

VLADIMIR. Healing leaves from the Land of No Return.

ADVISOR. *(taking leaves)* Your Majesty, earlier I summoned the physician from Gorki. He will administer the remedy.

CZAR. The remedy is here. I will wait for no one. Rub it in immediately.

CZARINA. Dear, a little patience will…

CZAR. Patience! You must be blinder than I am to not see how patiently I have endured a darkness blacker than the inside of a bear's belly.

ADVISOR. I hear the doctor now. *(going to greet him)* Doctor.

(**PHYSICIAN** *enters.*)

PHYSICIAN. Zdravstvuite, Your Majesties. The leaves.

(**ADVISOR** *hands them to him.*)

Ahh. Amazing. I have only read about these, never seen them. Forgive me. My hands are still ringing with the cold. Now, I will need you to remain perfectly still, sire. Advisor. I will need your assistance in holding the royal eyelid open, like so, when I instruct you to. *(Demonstrates.)*

ADVISOR. Alright. I understand.

PHYSICIAN. First I will rub the leaves over the entire lid area.

CZAR. Nothing is happening! These can't be the right leaves.

PRINCES. But...

OLGA. Don't worry, they'll work, Father.

IRINA. I'm sure they will.

PHYSICIAN. Your Majesty, we are not done yet.

CZAR. Well, hurry up.

PHYSICIAN. Please Your Majesty. You must sit very still.

ADVISOR. Are you ready, Sire?

CZARINA. Of course he is. He's very calm, aren't you, dear?

CZAR. Yes, yes, yes, yes.

PHYSICIAN. Advisor, your assistance, please. I will extract some of the juice with a twist. Now, blink several times very quickly, your majesty.

CZAR. *(blinking)* Everything is still dark...

ALL. *(sounding disappointed)* Ohhhhhh...

CZAR. Now it's grey...

ALL. *(sounding a little hopeful)* Huuh?

CZAR. and blurry, swimming around, getting lighter.

ALL. *(gasping with hope)* Ahhhhh….

CZAR. Clearer, clearer. I can….I can see!

ALL. Brava!

PHYSICIAN. Congratulations!

CZARINA. Wonderful.

PRINCES AND PRINCESSES: Brava!

(Freeze.)

STORYTELLER 1. While the court was celebrating the return of the Czar's sight, poor Alexi awoke in the ditch, cold, shivering and blind.

ALEXI. Darkness. I must have blacked out. How did I get outside? It must be night. *(rubs eyes and tilts face up)* And yet I can feel the sun on my face. Now I remember. The drink. It must have been drugged. *(groping around)* No bag. Well, that's no surprise, but I have more leaves in my pockets. *(fishes some out)* Still here. Good. A chance to see if they work before I take them to the Czar. *(rubs them on eyes, blinks)* Hmmmm… *(rubs them again)* There. More than my vision is coming into clear focus. I see what those schemers have done. I must hurry back to the palace. *(rises and starts back)*

*(**LARISSA** enters.)*

STORYTELLER 2. When Alexi returned home he showed Larissa the healing leaves.

LARISSA. Husband, you are too late. Prince Vladimir and Prince Igor have already brought back the healing leaves and my father can now see. He has given them each a third of his kingdom. Nothing is left for us.

ALEXI. Do not worry. In time, everyone will see clearly.

*(**ALEXI** and **LARISSA** exit.)*

STORYTELLER 1. When the Queen of the Land Of No Return awoke, she realized that her ring had been removed.

QUEEN. My ring! The leaves from my tree are missing. I must fly over the land until I find out who took them. *(clapping hands and turning)*
One – let the light of the sun
Two – show me who
Three – took the leaves off my tree
Four – bring me to their door.
High above the land
I hear first hand
What is being said.
Whoever took my ring will soon be dead.

STORYTELLER 2. The Queen heard of the Czar who had miraculously been cured of his blindness. Immediately, she went to the palace.

(All unfreeze.)

QUEEN. I am the Queen of No Return. If you do not tell me how you were cured of your blindness, I will have my dragon destroy your kingdom.

CZAR. Dragon?

QUEEN. Dragon. In one fiery breath.

ADVISOR. Your Majesty, with your permission, may I explain?

CZAR. There is no other choice but *to* explain.

ADVISOR. Prince Vladimir and Prince Igor brought back some healing leaves.

QUEEN. *(to* **PRINCES***)* Healing leaves?

PRINCES. Yes, your majesty.

QUEEN. And where did you get these healing leaves?

VLADIMIR. We found them on a tree.

QUEEN. Where?

IGOR. In the forest.

QUEEN. Liars! I will call my dragon now!

VLADIMIR. Wait! We will tell.

IGOR. We took them from a poor man.

QUEEN. Who is this man?

PRINCES. We do not know.

QUEEN. Again, you are lying!

VLADIMIR. It's the truth.

IGOR. We swear, it's the truth.

CZARINA. I know who the man is.

CZAR. You? Who is he? Speak!

CZARINA. It is Alexi, the poor man who is married to our daughter, Larissa.

(All gasp in astonishment.)

QUEEN. Send for him!

ADVISOR. Immediately. *(Exits.)*

STORYTELLER 1. While the Queen of No Return and the royal family waited nervously, Alexi and Larissa arrived at the palace.

*(**ADVISOR, ALEXI** and **LARISSA** arrive.)*

QUEEN. What do you know about these leaves?

STORYTELLER 2. Alexi told the Queen the entire story. He told about the extra leaves that he stuffed into his pockets.

*(**VLADIMIR** and **IGOR** exchange worried glances.)*

ALEXI. And here is the ring that I removed from your finger while you were sleeping, your highness. *(gives her back the ring)*

QUEEN. And how did these two princes get the leaves from you?

ALEXI. When I came to the inn, they stole my bag and drugged me.

CZAR. Disgraceful!

QUEEN. As a reward for your courage and for your true heart, I will permit you to keep the leaves. Do svidaniya, good-bye. *(She leaves.)*

ALEXI. Thank you. Do svidaniya.

CZAR. Prince Igor, Prince Vladimir. Step forward.

IRINA. Please, Father, be merciful.

OLGA. Have pity, Father.

IRINA. Remember, we were the obedient daughters.

OLGA. The ones who married as you said we should.

CZAR. The kingdom that I have given you, I now take back. The bulk of your wealth will be divided among the poor peasants of this land so that they may become as strong as their hearts. Alexi.

ALEXI. Your majesty.

CZAR. I ask your forgiveness for having been blind. Blind to the truth that Larissa was able to see. That the poorest person may possess the richest of hearts. You and Larissa will come and live in the palace and will take over the rule of the kingdom. *(gasps from all)* For you have the wisdom to rule wisely.

STORYTELLER 1. And so they did. In every peasant hut, there was plenty of borscht and bread and the people of the kingdom prospered.

STORYTELLERS. And all people lived in harmony.

(All dance Russian dance.)

(curtain)

GLOSSARY

Do svidaniya – (*duh svee-dah-nee-ye*) Good-bye.

Nah zdoroviya – (*na stro via*) To your health.

Zdravstvujtye – (*zdrah-stvooy-tee* – the first letter "v" in Zdravstvujtye is silent.) Hello.

TOPICS FOR DISCUSSION

What does the king mean when he says I was "blind to the truth"?

What can cause someone to not "see" clearly?

Why do you think most folktales and myths have almost impossible tasks that the protagonists must complete to achieve their goals?

JOHNNY APPLESEED IN CYBERSPACE

a folktale from the United States

Johnny Appleseed in Cyberspace was first presented by Metastages Theatre Centre on August 21, 1998 at the Pavilion Theatre, Penn State University, University Park, Pennsylvania. The production was directed by Mark Olsen and included the following cast:

KURT	Hari Venkat
MAYA	Christie McKinney
MATT	Darius Clement
JENN	Emily Fabre
SAM	Michael Powers
LISA	Lindi-Jo Mowrey
AUNT NELLIE	Keira Wilson
AUNT FLORRY	Kateri Polansky
JOHNNY APPLESEED	Toby Squier-Roper
AUNT MATTIE	Nilu Rahman
ABBY	Emily Weiner
SARAH	Marcella Vitale
CLARA	Elizabeth Houts
TILDY	Sarah Muscarella
PA	George Feasler
UNCLE EDGAR	Jonathan Lumley-Sapanski

CHARACTERS

KURT/CARLA
MAYA/MAX
MATT/ALLIE
JENN/JAKE
STACEY/SAM
LISA/LEE
UNCLE NATE/AUNT NELL
AUNT FLORRY
JOHNNY APPLESEED
AUNT MATTIE
ABBY/ABE
SARAH
CLARA
TILDY
PA/MA
UNCLE EDGAR/AUNT EDITH

*(Frozen tableau of kids playing at **KURT**'s computer. Music down, lights up: there is a sudden burst of computer game sounds, animated improvised talk. Very energetic into:)*

KURT. Let me play, Matt. I know how to beat this level.

MATT. Just a sec. Arhhh! What? Game over?!

KURT. I told you –

MATT. Wait –

KURT. Here, let me play.

MATT. Game over??

JENN. Hey guys.

STACEY. Are you done?

KURT. No!

JENN. It's getting late.

MAYA. Jenn's right. We have to get started on our homework project.

KURT. But I didn't get a chance to play yet.

LISA. Look, the teacher is like expecting a report tomorrow, ok? And I *need* a good grade.

KURT. Okay, okay. I'll run the first search.

JENN. Great.

LISA. So how're we supposed to find this Johnny Applejack dude?

JENN. Seed.

MAYA. What?

STACEY. Seed. Johnny Appleseed.

LISA. I like Applejacks.

GIRLS. *(The girls sing all together from the TV commercial.)* "I don't know why, I just do!"

KURT. Level four is really cool. The fireballs on this level turn into Flaming Sofas and –

JENN. Kurt!

KURT. Okay, okay. Geeez! So, we're looking for a guy named Appleseed, right?

MATT. Ms. Bailey said to use a search engine and look up all we can find on Johnny Appleseed.

STACEY. Isn't that the guy who went around and planted apple trees everywhere?

LISA. Yeah, that's right.

JENN. What else do we know about him? *(silence)* Where'd he come from? Who is he? Is Appleseeed his real name or as I suspect…

MATT. You hope –

JENN. Right. I HOPE it's a fake name. When did he live?

LISA. Why apples and not, like bananas or pears?

(Lights from screen change.)

KURT. Okay, I'm in.

MATT. All right.

KURT. Where should I begin?

JENN. Ahhh, at the beginning?

MATT. Everyone's a comedian. Let's start with Apple.

LISA. Why "Apple?" Why not "Johnny?"

KURT. Okay. "Johnny." WHAM! Wow! It says there are over 2 thousand entries!

LISA. We'll be here forever.

STACEY. What about using the first and last name together?

KURT. I'll try. Nothing.

MAYA. Maybe under 'American History' or 'trees' or something.

JENN. Folklore maybe?

(They look.)

Isn't Johnny Appleseed a folk hero from the pioneer days?

MATT. Thanks Einstein.

STACEY. Try folk hero.

KURT. Aye aye, Sarge. Whoa! Check this out. Cool graphics! Folk heroes.

> **(PIONEERS [AUNT NELL, AUNT FLORRY, TILDY, ABBY, SARAH, CLARA, UNCLE EDGAR, AUNT MATTIE]** *appear in frozen pose.)*

Now we're getting somewhere.

MATT. Bookmark that baby.

MAYA. Better get our notebooks.

> *(All agree and go to get notebooks, chatting. Lights change and **KURT** gets sucked into the computer and is gone.)*

LISA. Oh no. Oh no. How…like wow! Did you see that?

MATT. Stand back. Kurt! Kurt! Can you hear me?

STACEY. Holy cow.

MAYA. Calm down. Focus, guys. Panic will only get you so far.

LISA. Like, we better call 911.

JENN. Yeah, right. "Hello. Our friend just got sucked into the computer."

MATT. Look at the screen.

LISA. *(awed)* Freak out….

STACEY. What are all those weird words?

AUNT NELL. Each word below is like a key

TILDY. To unlock this cyber mystery.

ABBY. Enter one while holding hands

SARAH. And it will take you to new lands.

CLARA.: Attend to all the words you hear

UNCLE ED. And trust the path will soon be clear.

AUNT MATTIE. To find your friend you must proceed

ALL PIONEERS. To seek for Johnny Appleseed.

LISA. It wants us to, like, go after him.

MAYA. Yeah. But…

MATT. What have we got to lose? We gotta get Kurt back.

(All agree.)

STACEY. Each word below is a key…

MAYA. Look. One, two, three, four, five words…

JENN. And five of us!

LISA. Wow! This is weird. Totally weird.

JENN. Everyone, take a word and memorize it.

MATT. I'll take the first one, *bodacious.*

STACEY. I'll take the next one, *ramsquaddle.*

LISA. *Ab-squat-ulate.* Look everyone. I'm absquatulating.

(She squats down and waddles like a duck. All laugh.)

JENN. Mine is *ripstaver.*

MAYA. Mine is…Oh right, I can't even pronounce it. *Ob-flist- ti- cate,* I think.

STACEY. How are we going to find out what all these words mean. They're probably not even in the dictionary.

JENN & MATT. "Enter one while holding hands."

JENN. Let's line up and try.

MATT. Okay. I'll type in the first word. Give me your hand.

MAYA. Come on.

STACEY. Hope this works.

LISA. Hang on everyone.

JENN. Don't let go.

MATT. Here we go!

*(**MATT** hits enter button. There is a sound, a light change and the line enters cyberspace in slow motion. A man with a pot on his head beckons them.)*

JOHNNY A. Quit your turkey dreamin'. No need to make a mighty miration. Get on the hookworm hustle, and follow me.

(As he speaks, he begins to pantomime climbing over rocks and bushes. Kids follow.)

LISA. It's hard to hustle through all these berry brambles.

JOHNNY A. You're welcome to tread in my footsteps if you can spraddle far enough.

ALL. Spraddle?

JOHNNY A. Like this.

(He demonstrates wide step. Kids follow.)

(Softly rising sound of a wagon train song. Possibly "This Land is your Land.")

JOHNNY A. We're almost there. The folks here will give you such a teetotal welcome, you'll be grinning like a baked possum in no time.

*(As **JOHNNY** exits, song becomes louder.)*

(When the lights restore we see a wagon train campsite. A group of young people are playing games, and others are occupied with various activities – whittling, sewing, carrying off buckets. One young person is churning butter and singing in rhythm:)

STACEY. Where are we?

MATT. Looks like a – a wagon train.

MAYA. That means we…

JENN. We're time warped about 200 years.

LISA. Far out!

ABBY. Churn butter churn

Sarah's at the gate

waiting for a johnnycake.

AUNT MATTIE. *(ringing a bell)* Time to get ready for supper everyone.

AUNT NELL. Mighty glad for that news! I'm so hungry my belly thinks my throat's been cut. Look here Mattie. We got some new young'uns. Must have joined us from down the wagon train.

AUNT MATTIE. Well, welcome. Well, I see a heap o' stir and no biscuits around here. Everybody to your chores! *(to modern kids)* You're just in time. Best help gather wood for the fire. *(She goes off to other chores.)*

(as they gather wood with the other young people:)

---

*Please see Music Use Note on Page 3.

MATT. So, what are we having to eat?

ABBY. Johnnycake and beans.

STACEY. What's johnnycake?

SARAH. It's really a journey cake…a kind of corn bread for traveling.

LISA. I like cornbread with chili dogs.

CLARA. They eat dogs where you come from?

LISA. Not real dogs…just…sort of a sausage.

MAYA. Listen. Have you guys seen a kid named Kurt?

JENN. He was wearing a *(describe)*…

TILDY. No, but there's a passle of folks who just joined the train and if anyone would know, I reckon it'd be Aunt Florry.

CLARA. *(elbowing other pioneer children)* Come here. Say, have you heard this? Jake and Jess and Pinchme went out for a swim.

SARAH. Jake and Jess got drowned.

ABBY. Who was saved?

LISA. *(brightly)* Pinchme! *(She suddenly gets it. Groans with others.)* Ahhh.

MAYA. A rattlesnake!

(Screams from modern kids. They run.)

Boy was that ever scary!

SARAH. You've never seen a rattler before?

MAYA. No!

CLARA. Just gotta watch where you put your hands and feet.

TILDY. But you can't worry yourself into a washboard over it.

MATT. A washboard?

ABBY. You know….full of wrinkles. *(All laugh.)*

PA. *(entering)* You children sure are all fired up.

SARAH. We saw a fistful of rattler, Pa.

PA. Don't you know a rattlesnake can make a mighty good friend? *(winks at the others)*

STACEY. *(in disbelief)* Friend?

(Story is being pantomimed as it is told.)

PA. I was riding through Rip Shin Thicket one day and saw a rattler stuck under a stone.

TILDY. Yup, he got off his horse and started to kill it, but…

PIONEER KIDS. Tildy!

TILDY. Sorry.

PA. So I pushed the rock off the rattler and went home.

TILDY. But all the way back he kept hearing this funny sound behind him. *(grabs a piece of rope and wiggles it like a snake)*

PIONEER KIDS. Tildy!

TILDY. Alright, alright.

PA. Well, I looked back and saw that snake following right along behind me.

TILDY. Followed him right into his cabin.

PA. You want to tell it?

TILDY. As a matter of fact, I do. So Pa gave it a dish of milk. That snake lapped it up to the last drop. You could just see the gratitude in its eyes. Slept under the bed. Then one day -

CLARA. Not day. Night. There was a commotion and Pa grabbed his gun and said "show yourself –

SARAH. No, he said, "Better make yourself known or I'm likely to shoot."

PA. A voice yelled, "For Pete's sake, get this thing off me!" That rattler had wrapped itself around the leg of the man who was gonna rob me, and the leg of a table and was rattling its tail for the sheriff.

(Everyone chuckles.)

LISA. Is that really true?

PA. True as any tall tale.

ABBY. *(to **STACEY**)* Those funny lookin' britches of yours need mendin'.

CLARA. Probably got torn on a branch while you were hot-footing away from that rattler.

STACEY. It might be easier just to get some new pants at the store.

(Everyone laughs.)

SARAH. Is that how they do it where you come from?

TILDY. Finding a store on the trail is harder than climbing a peeled sapling heels upward.

ABBY. You have to live with what you got and what you can make.

CLARA. That's why women's hands are always busy as a bumblebee in a bucket of tar.

SARAH. You're either spinning, knitting, stitching or patching and that's only the half of it.

PA. That's for sure. Life is short and full o' blisters. Come, we'll have you fixed up in no time.

MAYA. Say, we're looking for Johnny Appleseed.

PIONEER KIDS. Johnny Appleseed?

SARAH. Here's Uncle Edgar!

PIONEER KIDS. Hi Uncle Edgar.

UNCLE ED. *(enters wiping hands on rag)* Sure hope the wagon wheel's not bodaciously ruint.

MATT. That's my word. What does bodacious mean?

UNCLE ED. Means "completely." Means we aren't movin' on till its fixed. Can also mean "bold." What's the matter? Where's yer schoolin'?

JENN. We just never learned that particular word.

(momentary awkward pause)

UNCLE ED. You're not the Watson brood are ya?

MAYA. Ah, no sir...we're...

UNCLE ED. Well, good. Clara, run and try to find some axle grease quick as an alligator can chew a puppy.

(CLARA exits.)

STACEY. What is it with these people and reptiles?

JENN. Listen!

UNCLE ED. Well, I'll be hornswaggled. Why don't we have a hoe-down. Can't go anywhere, so we might as well kick up some dust with a little light foot, eh?

(Others enter humming and clapping.)

Are the pickers and pluckers ready?

ALL. Sure are.

UNCLE ED. Come on.

(to the limberjack – wooden jointed doll on a platform that he jumps on making a tapping rhythm)

Jack, you know what to do?

AUNT FLORRY. Does a squirrel know a hickory nut from an acorn?

*(Limberjack rhythm instrument is put into action. Song starts along with impromptu square dance. **PIONEER KIDS** get some of the modern day kids to join in. Everyone sings including a group of square dancers who form a square and dance. Others are picking, plucking, strumming their instrument or doing hambone rhythms. A limberjack doll keeps rhythm. Solo lines may be assigned to some song lines if appropriate.)*

SONG.

1. Lost my partner, what'll I do?
Lost my partner, what'll I do?
Lost my partner, what'll I do?
Skip to my Lou, my darlin'.

Chorus:
Skip, skip, skip to my Lou,
Skip, skip, skip to my Lou,
Skip, skip, skip to my Lou,
Skip to my Lou, my darlin'.

2. I'll get another one, better than you, (3x)
Skip to my Lou, my darlin'.
(Chorus)

   3. Flies in the buttermilk, shoo, fly, shoo (3x)
      Skip to my Lou, my darlin'.
      (Chorus)

   4. Little red wagon painted blue, (3x)
      Skip to my Lou, my darlin'.
      (Chorus)

      (Everyone laughs and applauds.)

LISA. Wow, that's really cool.

      (PIONEERS *look at her strangely.)*

MAYA. She means she liked it.

LISA. Totally! It rhymes just like rap songs.

AUNT MATTIE. Rap songs?

STACEY. Yeah, you know:
      Yo check it.
      Word
      Sound
      Power
      Rhyme.
      My flow is infinite like space and time.
      The words spin around like the hands on a clock.
      Tic tic toc
      Hip to the hop.

      (Modern day kids join in chorus with dance moves and mouth beats.)

      Tic tic toc
      Hip to the hop (2x)

      (PIONEERS *are looking at them like they are from Mars.)*

JENN. It's a computer game actually where you make up your own rap…

AUNT FLORRY. Com-whater? You better snow again, I don't catch your drift.

MATT. It's sort of hard to explain…a computer is a…Jenn, use your noodle and tell em.

AUNT MATTIE. Noodle! Now that puts me in mind of Paul Bunyan and the macaroni farm.

PIONEER KIDS. Oh good!

AUNT FLORRY. Why don't we swap a story or two while the beans and johnnycake cook.

(Everyone gathers happily for storytelling.)

AUNT MATTIE. Don't be skittish now, grab a perch. Make some room now for our guests from…well, where are you from exactly?

UNCLE ED. Must be somewhere East with clothes like that.

MATT. Well not exactly..

JENN. That's right. From up East in Pennsylvania *(replace location with your own)*. Have you seen a kid named Kurt?

AUNT FLORRY. Nobody but you has joined us since the Cumberland Road. Cumberland Road is near Paul Bunyan country and Babe, his big blue ox.

MODERN KIDS. *(mouth silently, looking at each other)* Big blue ox?

AUNT FLORRY. Bunyan and some friends got together and decided to raise some macaroni.

SARAH. And some spaghetti too.

UNCLE ED. Macaroni, spaghetti. Easy enough for a ripstaver like Paul Bunyan.

JENN. Ripstaver! That's my word. What's a ripstaver?

*(**PIONEERS** laugh.)*

AUNT MATTIE. Now, now. These fine children are from back East and may not know about some things we know. You see a ripstaver is…well, ya think John Henry, Pecos Bill, you know, heroes.

LISA. Like Spider Man. *(substitute local hero)*

(Everyone looks at her.)

CLARA. Who?

JENN. Doesn't matter. So. Mr. Bunyan was raising…. *(clears throat)* pasta?

SARAH. What?

JENN. Macaroni?

AUNT FLORRY. That's right. Until they hit crop failure.

ABBY. It was terrible.

AUNT NELLIE. During the hard times, the demand for macaroni got way ahead of the supply. All that cheese piling up and no noodles to mix it with.

AUNT F. One crop after another totally ramsquaddled.

STACEY. Ramsquaddle! That's my word. What's it mean?

UNCLE ED. You can be crushed, demolished, beaten or ramsquaddled.

AUNT NELLIE. And not one of 'em feels a mite better than the other.

MATT. Well we're ramsquaddled if we don't find Johnny Appleseed. Does anyone know where he is?

LISA. You see our friend Kurt got sucked into a computer and…

MAYA. Lisa, I don't think

LISA. And we kinda time warped –

UNCLE EDGAR. What kind of crazy stranger folk are ya anyway….

AUNT FLORRY. Clarry, go get Pa.

JENN. Let's get out of here!

SARAH. They're getting away.

(Momentary chase as the group tries to gather hands together long enough to transfer away. They finally manage it.)

LISA. "Absquatulate." Group – "Absquatulate."

*(Lights change. **PIONEERS** fade back and exit as modern day group arrives at another location. They run in and see a single, lone individual, the one with the pot on his head who sits in eerie calm.)*

STACEY. Oh, hello again.

JOHNNY A. Now I ask myself, "What could make a passle of young 'uns absquatulate quicker than a flash of lightening?

MAYA. *(hoping to discover meaning)* Absquatulate – we…ah.. do a lot of that.

JOHNNY A. Do you now?

MATT. Look, we don't need any more rattlers, or "square" dancing or johnnycake…

JOHNNY A. Well, johnnycake's about my favorite thing side from apples. You like apples?

JENN. Sure we like apples.

JOHNNY A. Take these back where you came from and plant 'um.

(He gives them a pouch of seeds, which one of them puts in their pocket.)

STACEY. Sure, thanks, but have you seen a dude named Kurt. He was –

JOHNNY A. Six, slick, slim saplings.

LISA. What?

JOHNNY A. Betcha can't say that five times in a row.

MAYA. What was it again?

JOHNNY A. Six slick, slim saplings. Say it five times in a row and I'll answer all your questions.

MATT. Go ahead Jenn.

JENN. Six slick sim shaplings.

*(They laugh. **MATT** tries it and messes up.)*

JOHNNY A. Aw, don't worry. I'm just trying to obflisticate you.

MAYA. Hey! That's my word. Obflisticate. What does it mean? I'm confused.

JOHNNY A. Yes, you're obflisticated.

MAYA. I am? I don't get it. Oh! I'm confused….

JENN. Obflisticated.

MAYA. That was the last word on our list.

JOHNNY A. Well, I gotta head out West. No time for jaybird jabber. *(starts to exit)*

MATT. Wait! What about Kurt?

MATT. Have you seen our friend Kurt?

JOHNNY A. Maybe I have, maybe I haven't.

STACEY. This isn't a joke, sir. It's serious.

JOHNNY A. Run away.

LISA. What?

JOHNNY A. Absquatulate means, "to run away."

JENN. Did Kurt absquatulate?

JOHNNY A. You'll find him soon enough.

ALL. How?

JOHNNY A. To return with Kurt from whence you came
Just hold your hands and say my name.

So long, folks. Remember, an apple a day….

(He exits. They call out and protest with "Wait! Come back!" but to no avail.)

LISA. Bummer.

STACEY. Come on. Let's do as he said. Here, hold hands. Come on.

(They hold hands.)

MATT. But what's his name?

JENN. Think about it. All the stuff he said. He must be Johnny Appleseed.

*(Lights change. Restore to room with computer. They are all standing together with **KURT** sitting at desk. They are excited and all talk at once.)*

KURT. Chill! Not all at once. What's going on?

MAYA. While we were looking for you, we finally found that ole ripstaver Johnny Appleseed, but before that –

STACEY. Before that, we met up with this cool wagon train and nearly stepped on a rattlesnake and –

MATT. And when we started talking about computers, the pioneers got bodacious…

JENN. So we had to absquatulate…and we came upon this dude who was trying to obflisticate us, but it was really…

ALL. It was really Johnny Appleseed.

KURT. Johnny Appleseed? I remember now…

ALL. *(sighing with relief)* Yeah…

KURT. You guys were there…and you…and you.

ALL. Right.

KURT. …and little Toto too! *(They all laugh.)*

ONE WHO HAS SEEDS. But we really did meet him. We were there and… *(stuffs hands in pocket)*

KURT. This virtual reality thing is over the edge.

ONE WHO HAS SEEDS. Look! Holy cow. I can't believe it. Seeds!

KURT. *(looking at the seeds)* Freaky. That does it. From now on, it's caffeine free soda for you guys.

(They pretend to mob him and tickle him and they all burst into a flurry of teasing and protesting and then FREEZE. Music up, lights down.)

(curtain)

TOPICS FOR DISCUSSION

If there were a reality show where you could go back in history and spend a week there, what time and place would you most like to experience?

Think about everything you do during a 24 hour period, from getting up in the morning to going to bed and sleeping through the night. What do you think would be the hardest parts of being on a pioneer wagon train?

Are there parts of pioneer life in the 1800's that you think would be fun or interesting?

SEARCH FOR PERFECTION

A folktale from Nigeria

Search for Perfection was first presented by Metastages Theatre Centre on August 16, 2002 at the Pavilion Theatre, Penn State University, University Park, Pennsylvania. The cultural resource advisor was Dr. Clemente Abrokwa. The production was directed by Mark Olsen and included the following cast:

JENN . . . . Meghan Hart

FENSKY . . . . Michael Green

KATE . . . . Annie Boggess

SMITTY . . . . Brian Kowalski

SHEPHERDESS . . . . Krysta Koubek

BIRD/MATADI . . . . Lauren Schloss

PRINCE TUNDE . . . . Benjamin Carlsen

KING . . . . Steven Tippeconnic

ROYAL ADVISOR . . . . Brad Woodman

ROYAL PHYSICIAN . . . . Aaron Kaye

PRINCESS KEIKO, SERVANT 2 . . . . Seungwon Chung

PRINCESS KATARINA, SERVANT 1 . . . . Cassie van Stolk-Cooke

PRINCESS SHANTA, LION . . . . Amy Copley

PRINCESS ROSA, SNAKE . . . . Emily Woodard

PRINCESS SHADE, SNAKE . . . . Kara Smith

PRINCESS OSHUPA, GIANT . . . . Christina Carpenter

PRINCESS INORA . . . . Karen Jovanis

MONSTER . . . . Minu Nahm

CHARACTERS

JENN
FENSKY
KATE
SMITTY
SHEPHERDESS
BIRD/MATADI
PRINCE TUNDE
KING/QUEEN
ROYAL ADVISOR
ROYAL PHYSICIAN
PRINCESS KEIKO
PRINCESS KATARINA
PRINCESS SHADE
PRINCESS OSHUPA
MONSTER
PRINCESS INORA
SNAKES 1& 2, LION, GIANT, SERVANTS TO PRINCESS OSHUPA

(lunchtime at school.)

SMITTY. So, Fensky, who are you taking to the dance?

FENSKY. No one yet.

KATE. But it's next week.

FENSKY. Now *she's* definitely a prime candidate. *(points to passerby)*

JENN. Not a chance, Fensky, she's already got a date.

FENSKY. "Carrots" called and asked me to go.

SMITTY. Hey, she's got brains *and* beauty.

FENSKY. Naw. Not my type. Laughs like a chipmunk.

JENN. Hopeless, totally hopeless.

SMITTY. Hey, ladies, it goes both ways. I've heard you dissing us guys.

KATE. Well, when you finally find Miss Perfect, I hope she's not a Princess Oshupa.

FENSKY. A who what?

KATE. Didn't you read about her in Lit. class?

FENSKY. No.

JENN. It's a story from Africa

KATE. *(laughing)* You didn't have a past life in Africa a few hundred years ago, did you?

JENN. 'Cause this story is definitely you, Fensky.

FENSKY. What do you mean?

JENN. Tell him, Kate.

KATE. Well, it all started in Nigeria in this beautiful palace. There was this dude named

PRINCE. Tunde. *(pronounced Tune-day)*

JENN. Handsome was his middle name.

KATE. Outside his palace sat a shepherdess, who tended the royal sheep.

JENN. Beautiful she wasn't. But she played lovely music and she had a secret.

(Music. A lowly **SHEPHERDESS** *appears followed by her pet bird. The bird perches nearby and sings.)*

SHEPHERDESS. *(sings)* Wood cutter, wood cutter, go tell my mother,

Wood cutter, wood cutter go tell my father,

Everyone lives at home but me. My life was stolen.

BIRD. Your song, my song. It makes no difference. Prince Tunde pays no more heed to us than to the wind.

SHEPHERDESS. You are right, my friend.

BIRD. But here comes music the Prince will listen to, for it brings royal beauties to the palace. Princesses from near and far. Every one of them accomplished, talented and beautiful. Each one hoping to become Prince Tunde's bride.

(All **PRINCESSES** *except* **OSHUPA** *dance on.)*

SHEPHERDESS. Beautiful, yes, but who among them will have the perfection that the Prince insists upon?

BIRD. If Prince Tunde could only see into your heart. He would understand the truth.

(PRINCE, KING/QUEEN, ADVISOR *and* **PHYSICIAN** *enter. Dancers bow.)*

ADVISOR. Bawoni! *(pronounced bow-o-knee)* Royal highnesses from the far reaches of the world. Welcome to our royal court.

KING/QUEEN. Look my son. Such beauties! Long fine hands, lovely faces, full every grace.

PRINCE. Yes Mother/Father. Beautiful, but which one is without flaw. My bride must be without the slightest imperfection.

KING/QUEEN. One maiden after another. You reject them all.

PRINCE. And for good reason. She who comes before me perfect as the full moon will be my bride.

KING/QUEEN. My son, even the moon waxes and wanes.

PRINCE. Proceed. Who will be first? You! *(He points.)*

PRIN. KEIKO. Your royal highness. Konichiwa. *(She bows low.)*

ADVISOR. *(consulting scroll)* Presenting Princess Keiko *(pronounced Kay-koh)* from the land of the rising sun. She has studied the healing arts of the ancients, and she is skilled in the exotic cuisine of the Far East.

PRIN. KEIKO. *(extracting an herb)* Your Majesty, this herb comes from a rare plant found in the far reaches of the mountains. A few drops will remedy all pain of muscles, joints, wounds, stings, boils...

PRINCE. *(taking herb)* Yes, yes. Thank you. What delicacies have you brought?

PRIN. KEIKO. A confection that takes seventy days to prepare. Each sweet is flavored by the pollen of 3000 night blooming flowers that blossom but once a year.

PRINCE. Rather small. *(eats one)* Quite tasty.

*(takes handful and passes rest to **KING/QUEEN**)*

PRIN. KEIKO. If your Majesty would but let the flavor linger on the palate a bit....

PRINCE. Physician. Put her to your test.

PHYSICIAN. As you wish, Your Majesty. This way Princess.

(takes her to be examined)

PRINCE. *(licking fingers)* Are there more?

KING/QUEEN. Quite a few. But shouldn't you let those delicacies digest first?

PRINCE. No, give them here.

(PHYSICIAN *brings back the* **PRINCESS.**)

PHYSICIAN. As rare a specimen as the exotic gifts she bears, Your Majesty.

PRINCE. Completely without blemish?

PHYSICIAN. Completely. Save for the faint ghost of a scar on her thumb.

PRIN. KEIKO. A mere scratch, Your Majesty, from a thorn lodged in my thumb while collecting herbs in the mountains to concoct an ointment.

PRINCE. Unfortunate indeed, but I must reject you. I cannot marry someone who is less than perfect. Farewell, Princess Keiko. *(She starts to leave.)* Oh, and could you send some more of these little sweets tomorrow? I quite fancy them. *(She leaves.)*

ADVISOR. *(consulting a scroll)* Presenting Princess Katarina who travels here from across the wide ocean. She will recite poetry for your listening pleasure.

PRIN. KATARINA. Your Highness, for many years I have studied literature and poetry from around the world. I speak seven languages and to give the sweetness of honey to your ears, I will recite some poetry. The first one is in French. La belle lune de nui.....

PRINCE. Skip the French.

PRIN. KATARINA. Then a sonnet by the English poet, William Shakespeare.

Let me not to the marriage of true minds

Admit impediments. Love is not love

which alters when it alteration finds.

Or bends with the remover to remove.

Oh no! It is an ever-fixed mark

That looks on tempests and is never shaken.

It is the star to every wandering bark,

Whose worth's unknown, although his height be taken.

Love's not Time's fool, though rosy lips and cheeks

Within his bending sickle's compass come.

Love alters not with his brief hours and weeks,

But bears it out even to the edge of doom.

PRINCE. *(interrupts her)* Thank you, thank you, Princess Katarina. The Royal Physician will examine you.

(**PRINCESS KATARINA** *and* **PHYSICIAN** *move to the side.)*

KING/QUEEN. Let the music continue. Perhaps, my son, the dancing will sway your heart.

(*Music as Princesses dance.* **PHYSICIAN** *returns with* **PRINCESS KATARINA**.)

PHYSICIAN. Smooth of skin. Clear of eye. Strong and limber.

KING/QUEEN. Surely, my son, this is a match.

PRINCE. Physician, you found no nick or mark?

PHYSICIAN. Not worth noting your majesty.

PRINCE. Speak!

PHYSICIAN. So small a mark I thought it must be only a speck of matter in my own eye.

PRIN. KATARINA. Your Majesty, when I was a child, I had a rambunctious pet, a bear cub orphaned in hunt, who in the tumble of play did snag its claw on the nape of my neck.

PHYSICIAN. Well hidden your majesty. Unnoticeable.

PRINCE. A pity. But she will not do. Goodbye, Princess Katarina.

(**PRINCESS KATARINA** *leaves.*)

KING/QUEEN. Advisor, present the next princess.

ADVISOR. Princess Shanta from India, the land of curry and spices. Princess Shanta has the gift of one who sees with a third eye.

PRIN. SHANTA. Namaste, Your Majesty. Allow me to read your fortune, your future, your heart.

PRINCE. (*laughing*) My fortune? There is no secret in that. Read my heart.

PRIN. SHANTA. (*closes her eyes*) Your heart is… Your heart is hard… (*opens her eyes and quickly tries to change her words*) Hard to see, that is.

PRINCE. You promise much and deliver nothing.

KING/QUEEN. Patience my son. The future, Princess Shanta. Read the future.

PRIN. SHANTA. *(closes her eyes again)* Your mirror does not reflect clearly, Your Majesty. Do you know why? Because rust has begun to cover it. It needs to be cleaned. You do not see what is before your eyes. Arm yourself with your sharpest sword for you will soon be deceived by what appears to be splendor.

PRINCE. How dare you!

PRIN. SHANTA. You do not heed the words that warn you. Your ears are open only to what they want to hear. You do not let in the one who would set you free. The fire awaits you. It is burning even now.

PRINCE. Take this babbler away!

PRIN. SHANTA. Your majesty, I only tell what I see. Namaste.

(She bows and exits.)

ADVISOR. From the land of blue skies and warm people, Princess Rosa Esmerelda Maria Consuela, Matilda, Theresa. She is a keeper of stories.

PRIN. ROSA. Hola, Your Majesty. *(She moves in dance-like motion as she speaks.)* Perhaps the fire of my words will warm you. For I am a story keeper. One who keeps the flame of memory burning through time and space. One who holds the past. The ancestors whisper their secrets to me. They pass their stories down through the ages so we will know where we come from, who we are and who we will become. Would you like for me to tell you stories of the mountain people?

PRINCE. I'm not interested.

PRIN. ROSA. Or stories of those who live by the sea and talk of tides, and stars and wind and seasons.

PRINCE. I don't want a wife whose tongue flaps like a flock of birds.

PRIN. ROSA. And I don't want a husband whose ears are deaf to the wisdom of our ancestors.

PRINCE. What impertinence! Be gone!

(PRINCESS ROSA exits.)

KING/QUEEN. *(exasperated with son)* Please, who is next?

ADVISOR. Princess Shade *(pronounced Shah-day).*

PRIN. SHADE. I have studied the sciences as well as the arts of dance and music. First, for your enlightenment I shall expound on the theory of mineralogy.

(PRINCE rolls his eyes.)

Of great interest to scholars is the category of polymorphic minerals which include quartz, tridymite....

PRINCE. Enough! This is not a classroom, Princess. I seek a bride, not a school teacher.

ADVISOR. Then perhaps a song or dance.

PRINCE. Let her show her dance. *(or sing or play an instrument)*

PRIN. SHADE. As it pleases Your Majesty. *(She performs.)*

PRINCE. Thank you, Princess Shade. Physician, examine her.

PRIN. SHADE. By myself I confess, Your Majesty, to a tiny scar on my left toe. *(Holds out foot.)*

(PHYSICIAN looks at it.)

PHYSICIAN. Hardly visible, Sire.

PRIN. SHADE. Climbing some rocks during the harvest festival.

PRINCE. *(shakes his head)* Never.

KING/QUEEN. My son, even the patience of our ancestors has limits.

PRINCE. She will not do. *My* bride must be perfect.

(PRINCESS SHADE is escorted out by the PHYSICIAN. KING/QUEEN and ADVISOR look at each other and sigh with frustration. Sound of the shepherdess's tune.)

What is that noise?

ADVISOR. *(looks out)* Your Majesty, it is a tune played by the shepherdess.

PRINCE. *(looking)* Day and night, she plays. The melancholy of her music is matched only by the discord of her looks and that ridiculous bird of hers.

ADVISOR. Unfortunate to be sure.

PRINCE. Unfortunate for us to have our senses so offended. Dirty, wretched, scarred.

KING/QUEEN. Her scars are wounds from wild animals that attacked our flock which she valiantly defended. Take care whom you cast aside, my son. Misfortune is not particular. It can change the life of a pauper or a prince in an instant.

(Drums or trumpets sound.)

ADVISOR. What is that sound? *(looks off)* A royal entourage!

KING/QUEEN. *(looking off)* Surely someone of great wealth and power!

*(****PHYSICIAN*** *returns.)*

ADVISOR. Look, servants bearing gifts.

SERVANT 1. *(entering and kneeling before the* **PRINCE***)* Your Majesty, a gift from Princess Oshupa. *(pronounced Oh-shoe-pah).*

SERVANT 2. *(entering and kneeling before the* **PRINCE***)* Your Majesty, a gift from Princess Oshupa.

OSHUPA. *(entering and bowing to* **PRINCE***)* Your Majesty, I am Princess Oshupa from the golden kingdom. My love for you shall be as flawless as I am.

ADVISOR. The Physician is ready when you are, Princess Oshupa.

PHYSICIAN. This way, your Majesty.

*(****PHYSICIAN*** *and* ***PRINCESS*** *move aside.)*

PRINCE. *(opening one of the gifts)* What treasures!

KING/QUEEN. A gift of opulence!

ADVISOR. I will hold them for safe-keeping, your Majesty. *(takes gifts)*

PHYSICIAN. *(turning back in with* **PRINCESS***)* Not a single blemish, Sire. From head to toe, perfection.

*(****ADVISOR*** *and* ***KING/QUEEN*** *gasp in disbelief.)*

PRINCE. Let the wedding preparations begin. *(applause)* Come, my perfect bride-to-be. We shall plan the feast.

(All exit.)

FENSKY. Hey, picture perfect chick!

SMITTY. So…they got married and lived happily ever after?

JENN. Hardly.

KATE. The wedding lasted for seven days and seven nights.

JENN. When the wedding was over, Princess Oshupa took Prince Tunde to visit her kingdom in Okuta *(pronounced Oh-coo-ta).*

*(Enter **ROYAL COUPLE** and **SERVANTS** ready to travel.)*

JENN. They were just about to leave when…

*(**SHEPHERDESS** and **BIRD** enter.)*

SHEPHERDESS. Your Royal Highness, please accept my instrument as a wedding gift. *(offers musical instrument)*

PRINCE. What would I want with that? Be gone! *(looks at **PRINCESS** and laughs)*

SHEPHERDESS. I beg you, Sire, if you are ever in danger, you need only to play my song and help will come.

PRINCE. Who are you, lowly worm, to tell me what to do?

OSHUPA. Who dares to anger you, my Prince?

PRINCE. This shepherdess.

OSHUPA. Have her banished.

PRINCE. Go back to my sheep or you will be punished.

*(**SHEPHERDESS** bows, but as **PRINCE** turns back to **PRINCESS**, she slips the instrument into his pouch and signals the **BIRD** to follow them.)*

PRINCE. Now, my love, let us be off. I'm eager to see the kingdom from which such perfection comes.

OSHUPA. You shall experience a land far beyond the limits of your imagination.

*(**SERVANTS** rise and entourage begins the journey. Traveling music. They stop.)*

OSHUPA. Let us stop and rest here a while. *(motions the **SERVANTS** to kneel before her)*

PRINCE. *(sitting down)* What would you have with the servants?

OSHUPA. It does not concern you. Relax and rest from your journey.

PRINCE. *(smiles and leans back)* What should I expect but perfect understanding from my perfect bride.

OSHUPA. *(Removes her royal robe and tiara, revealing herself dressed in plain clothes. She gives the royal garments to the* **SERVANTS.** *Then she begins to remove her jewels.)* Here, take these and return them to their proper owners.

*(***BIRD*** circles ***PRINCE*** and trills as if to warn him.)*

BIRD. Trrrou, trrrou, trrrou.

PRINCE. Why do you shed your royal robe and jewels?

OSHUPA. Do not ask questions. To the flowers, I returned the color of my robe to the sun. The sparkle of my jewels to the stars.

*(***SERVANTS*** depart.)*

PRINCE. *(standing)* Your perfection needs no royal robes.

OSHUPA. Then let us continue our journey.

(They walk. More music.)

*(***BIRD*** circles ***PRINCE*** and trills.)*

BIRD. Trrrou, trrrou, trrrou.

OSHUPA. Wait here. I will return soon. *(She exits.)*

PRINCE. *(sits)* Ah, this kingdom is a far journey from my home. But if its splendor is equal to my bride, it will be worth the effort.

*(A ***MONSTER*** enters and does a menacing dance.* ***PRINCE*** rises frightened.)*

Who are you?

MONSTER. Spoiled son of a stupid Queen/King. You wanted a perfect wife. Well, here I am. Teeth perfectly sharp. Bountiful hair. *(strokes its fur)* Eyes perfectly bright. And my home, perfectly hidden from all who would look to find you. Soon I will roast you and feed your bones to my piranhas. For now you have time to think of your foolish vanity. I will return post haste.

(**MONSTER** *exits.*)

PRINCE. What a fool I've been. I would have been better off married to the lowly shepherdess than to this monster. At least she cares about my well being. If I must die, however, I will die bravely as a prince should. But first I will write an apology to my mother/father. *(opens pack and discovers the shepherdess' instrument)* The instrument of the shepherdess. What did she say? If you are in danger, play my song. How did it go? A million times I must have heard that sad song.

(plays and sings)

Wood cutter, wood cutter, go tell my mother,

Wood cutter, wood cutter, go tell my father,

Everyone lives at home but me. My life has been stolen.

(**SHEPHERDESS** *enters at side of stage.* **BIRD** *flies back to* **SHEPHERDESS**.*)*

SHEPHERDESS. What news, my winged messenger?

BIRD. Prince Tunde turned away so many talented and lovely princesses because of a silly flaw.

SHEPHERDESS. And now?

BIRD. Princess Oshupa has turned back to into the monster that she really is. And worst of all, the monster plans to roast Prince Tunde and feed him to the piranhas.

SHEPHERDESS. I must act quickly.

(She runs toward palace and into the **ADVISOR** *who pushes* **SHEPHERDESS** *back.)*

I must speak the Queen/King immediately.

ADVISOR. Impossible.

SHEPHERDESS. But the Prince is in grave danger.

QUEEN/KING. *(entering with* **PHYSICIAN***)* What is it, Advisor?

ADVISOR. This shepherdess says your son is in danger, Your Majesty.

QUEEN/KING. *(laughing)* Nonsense! The Prince has married the richest and most beautiful Princess in the world and they have gone to her kingdom in Okuta. Go back to your sheep.

SHEPHERDESS. Then I must rescue him myself.

(She exits.)

PHYSICIAN. Poor girl. Where is this kingdom of Okuta?

ADVISOR. Come to think of it, I have never heard of this place.

KING/QUEEN. What? Then we must set off at once and make sure that my son is safe and happy.

*(**KING/QUEEN** exits.)*

PRINCE. *(sitting at side of stage, singing)*
Wood cutter, wood cutter, go tell my mother,
Wood cutter, wood cutter, go tell my father,
Everyone lives at home but me. My life has been stolen.

*(There is a sound of drums. **PRINCE** stands.)*

My Mother/Father! I hear her/his drummers.

*(**KING/QUEEN**, **ADVISOR** & **PHYSICIAN** enter but are intercepted by **MONSTER**.)*

MONSTER. *(laughing)* Come to save your son, foolish King/Queen? You are too late! Turn back while you still have breath in your body.

KING/QUEEN. Who are you?

MONSTER. Don't you recognize me? I am the perfect Princess of Okuta.

*(A sword is drawn but the **MONSTER** disappears.)*

ADVISOR. The monster has disappeared!

PHYSICIAN. What is going on?

*(They rush to look where the **MONSTER** has gone, but the **MONSTER** reappears behind them.)*

MONSTER. Freeze into stone forever!

*(**MONSTER** turns the **ADVISOR** and **PHYSICIAN** to stone.)*

Where are your defenders now?

(**KING/QUEEN** *turns back.*)

Join them, you fool!

(*Changes* **KING/QUEEN** *into stone, then turns on* **PRINCE.**)

Now my Prince, I, your perfect Princess, will scorch you with a blaze more fiery than passion.

SHEPHERDESS. *(entering)* Stop! The Prince will not die.

MONSTER. Who are you?

SHEPHERDESS. Don't you recognize me?

BIRD. *(flies around screeching)* And me? And me? And me?

MONSTER. Now I do. You are Inora *(ee-nora)*, Princess of the Noonday Sun.

SHEPHERDESS. And now I challenge you, Oshupa, evil Princess of Midnight. It was you who turned me into a scarred and lowly wretch.

BIRD. And changed me, her servant, into a bird.

SHEPHERDESS. I have waited seven years for this day.

(*She lunges at* **MONSTER** *who disappears and is replaced by a fierce lion. They battle until the Shepherdess chases the lion away.*)

FENSKY. So *now* the Prince and the Shepherdess get married and lived "happily ever after," right?

KATE. Wrong!

JENN. The lion soon morphed into this huge giant.

SMITTY. Giant!

FENSKY. This is so cliché. Battling lions and giants. Can't they be a little more original?

SMITTY. Come on, it's the ultimate extreme sports.

KATE. You want original, Fensky, what would you suggest?

JENN. Fear Factor challenges on Fraser Street?

KATE. Survivor Mt. Nittany? *(use a local landmark)*

FENSKY. How about a can-you-top this joke contest?

SMITTY. Jokes? You've got to be kidding.

FENSKY. Sure. *(takes fight stance)* Like,...okay, Princess Oshupa, this one will slay you. A kid walks into the house with a handful of dog doo. And he says to his mother, "look what I almost stepped in."

JENN & KATE. Ooooooo, GROSS!!!!!

JENN. Men and their toilet brain mentality!

KATE. Hey, how about this one. *(mimes parrying a sword)* Why do women's brains cost less than men's brains?

SMITTY. Beats me.

KATE. Because they're used!

FENSKY. Touché!

SMITTY. My turn. En garde. *(takes fight stance, then goes into joke)* How do you make a handkerchief dance?

JENN. I don't know. How *do* you make a handkerchief dance?

SMITTY. Put a little boogie in it!

FENSKY. *(laughs heartily)* Great joke!

KATE. *(not smiling)* Look who thinks it's funny.

JENN. Okay! Listen up. This is a lion and monster joke. How do you catch a unique animal?

SMITTY. I dunno.   **KATE.** How do you?   **FENSKY.** How?

KATE. You neek up on it.

FENSKY. *(groan)* So what happened with the Giant and the Shepherdess?

KATE. The Shepherdess and the Giant struggled for three days and three nights.

(Drums. **SHEPHERDESS** *chases the* **GIANT** *on, menacing it with a stick. They square off and a stylized fight ensues.)*

SHEPHERDESS. *(Whacks* **GIANT**. **GIANT** *staggers.)* Finally!

GIANT. Not quite. *(as* **GIANT** *backs off)* Look behind you, you wretch.

*(**SHEPHERDESS** turns and is confronted by a two-headed **SNAKE** which appears behind her.)*

SNAKES. *(Each line is repeated twice.)* Sorry to dissssappoint you Inora. Three timessss and you're out. Usssse your head Inora. *(**SNAKES** laugh.)* Ssss ssss sss.

(The **PRINCE** *begins to play the instrument.* **SNAKES** *pause to look at him and* **SHEPHERDESS** *attacks them.* **SNAKES** *slither off in fear.)*

SHEPHERDESS. I shall pursue you, evil Princess of Midnight, until it costs you both your heads! *(She rushes off in pursuit of the snakes.)*

PRINCE. *(leaps up)* I'll help you, Shepherdess!

BIRD. *(gets in his way)* Stop. She must resolve this by herself.

PRINCE. But she needs my help.

BIRD. Too late to help her now. It is her battle and she must fight it alone. Seven years ago the evil Oshupa put a spell on my mistress, the beautiful Princess Inora. Until Inora destroys Oshupa the spell will not be broken.

PRINCE. *(Turns to see frozen* **KING/QUEEN**, **ADVISOR** *and* **PHYSICIAN***.)* Look what I've done with my stupid quest for perfection. My Father/Mother is frozen like a rock and my faithful Shepherdess is in peril.

(The **PRINCE** *moves to the frozen* **KING** *and kneels in grief. A blood-curdling scream is heard in the distance.)*

BIRD. *(looking off)* The serpent has been slain! My mistress is returning.

(Backing on masked by the **SHEPHERDESS**' *cloak, we do not see until she turns around that it is* **PRINCESS INORA**.*)*

INORA. *(calling)* Help! Help me, my loyal friend.

BIRD. Here, your Majesty! Are you all right?

*(***BIRD** *removes the* **SHEPHERDESS**' *cape and each are transformed, the* **SHEPHERDESS** *into* **PRINCESS INORA** *and the* **BIRD** *into her Servant,* **MATADI***.)*

INORA. My loyal servant, Matadi. Our fortune is as changing as the seasons. Winged or on foot, you are by my side always.

MATADI. And always will remain. Even when you were a wretched Shepherdess and had nothing to eat but a bit of bread, you never failed to share with me. Though your appearance changed, your generous nature did not. Look, the Prince is grieving for all the trouble he has caused.

PRINCE. *(crosses to **PRINCESS INORA** and kneels)* Forgive me, Your Majesty, for I have wronged you.

INORA. *(to **PRINCE**)* Your tears, Sire, have cleansed both your heart and eyes. Now you begin to see clearly. Not all that shines is gold. Now you are able to see past mere outward appearances. And outward appearance never lasts – the small child grows taller, the smooth skin grows wrinkled, the hair grows gray. Quickly, Matadi, collect his tears. When the heart is profoundly changed, tears have the power to transform.

*(**MATADI** does.)*

PRINCE. You hold both my sorrow, my joy and my gratitude in your hand.

INORA. Sprinkle the stones with the tears. There is a sacredness in tears. They are not the mark of weakness, but of power. They speak more eloquently than ten thousand tongues. They are the messengers of overwhelming grief, of deep remorse and of unspeakable love.

MATADI. Yes, Your Majesty. At once. *(**MATADI** does.)*

(Music. Stones come to life and all are reunited.)

KATE. The royal family returned home. The wedding took place at once.

(Court freezes in formal pose.)

SMITTY. *(looks at his watch)* Hey guys, we're going to get killed too if we're late for Chemistry.

FENSKY. You see, this story proves my point!

JENN. What point.

FENSKY. Princess Eyore…

KATE. *(groaning)* Inora!

FENSKY. Yeah, Princess whatever turned out to be the hottest chick of them all!

JENN & KATE. *(looking at each other)* Hopeless. Totally hopeless.

SMITTY. Three times and you're out!

JENN. Turning down "Carrots" for the dance was one.

KATE. Your "hot chick" remark was two.

FENSKY. So I'm a pig. Whatever happened to them?

JENN. Well, Tunde and Inora lived together for many years. They had their problems, of course, but their life was good.

KATE. And Prince Tunde had finally learned that there is no such thing as perfection.

FENSKY. *(looking at the frozen tableau)* Perfect or not, I wish Inora would go to the dance with me.

SMITTY. Fensky!

KATE. KATE. Get outta here, Fensky!

JENN. You're hopeless!

(All chase him off hitting him on the head with books.)

(music and curtain)

PRODUCTION NOTES

The two-headed snake can be achieved by one actor with each arm in a snake-like sheath (footed stockings or colored tights) or African material sewn into a tube with mitten pouches for the hand to fit in and create a moving mouth. Alternatively, two actors can move choreographically as the snakes.

One way to portray the giant would be to drape an actor from head to toe in obscuring fabric and to achieve gigantic height with a large head mask attached to a long stick that also has a cloth drape that obscures the stick.

Alternate jokes can be used instead of the ones included.

TOPICS FOR DISCUSSION

What is perfection?

Are human beings capable of perfection?

What are some of the ways you can discover someone's inner qualities beyond their outward appearance?

Do you agree or disagree with Inora's statement that "When the heart is profoundly changed, tears have the power to transform"?

Do you think that tears can heal?

SONG OF THE SEA

A folktale from Finland

Song of the Sea was first presented by Metastages Theatre Centre on August 21, 1998 at the Pavilion Theatre, Penn State University, University Park, Pennsylvania. The cultural resource advisor was Ulla Mansikka-Weiner. The production was directed by the author and included the following cast:

STORYTELLER 1	Samantha Shoffner
STORYTELLER 2	Maria Romasco-Moore
STORYTELLER 3	Megan Decoteau
SORCERESS 1	Jenna Roy
SORCERESS 2	Stephanie Shoffner
SORCERESS 3	Rebecca Bleznak
PRINCE TUNDE	Megan Supina
LASS	Ian Boswell
KING	Emilie Dile
GOODY WOMAN	Scott Porterfield
JUKKA	Lisa Leventry
QUEEN	Shuja Haider
KEEPER OF THE WINDS	Asad Haider
TROLL OF THE TREASURE CHEST	Caroline Phillips
RIVER WOMAN	Samantha Bernecker
AURORA	Kathryn Freeman

CHARACTERS

STORYTELLER 1
STORYTELLER 2
STORYTELLER 3
SORCERESS 1
SORCERESS 2
SORCERESS 3
LASS/LAD
KING
GOODY WOMAN
QUEEN
KEEPER OF THE WINDS
TROLL OF THE TREASURE CHEST
RIVER ROWER
AURORA
LOUHI OF THE NORTHLAND

(**STORYTELLERS 1, 2, 3** *enter to music and place handi-work [basket of knitting, mending – socks, fishing nets – leather work, carving, etc.] on stage where they will sit for the rest of the play.* **STORYTELLER 2** *picks up ball of thick-stranded yarn from basket. The loose end of the ball of yarn trails all the way offstage. Slowly,* **STORYTELLER 2** *begins to wind the long strand of yarn onto the ball and soon, the cast members, holding onto the strand, one by one, appear from offstage as they are reeled onstage.*

STORYTELLER 1. Then came frost and sang its verses *(sits and picks up knitting)*

STORYTELLER 2. Other tales the wind delivered
On the sea waves songs came drifting *(winding the cord)*

STORYTELLER 3. Magic charms the birds have added
From the treetops' incantations *(sits and picks up mend-ing from basket)*

STORYTELLER 2. These I rolled up in a ball
Made a fitting yarn ball of them
In my basket put the yarn ball

STORYTELLER 1. Now we knit it into story, linking words for all to hear.

(Background music begins.)

STORYTELLER 2. Three sorceresses were traveling through Finland when night fell.

SORCERESS 1. Look. A small tupa.

SORCERESS 2. Let's see if the owner will put us up for the night. I don't fancy sleeping in the woods and being wakened by the wet muzzle of a slobbering elk.

SORCERESS 3. Call loudly, for the wind howls.

SORCERESS 1. Maybe wind. Maybe wolves.

SORCERESS 2. *(calls)* Helloooo.

LASS/LAD. *(carries a baby)* Hyvää iltaa. Good evening, good travelers.

SORCERESS 2. Good evening, lass/lad. We are sisters three seeking lodging.

LASS/LAD. I am sorely grieved. This very day, my dear mother died in childbirth. The babe is a ruddy cheeked boy/girl. But with my father away at sea and my mother gone, I am as churned about as butter. If you wouldn't mind sleeping in the sauna, you are welcome.

SORCERESS 3. Kiitos. Thank you. May your kindness be amply repaid.

(LASS/LAD leaves.)

STORYTELLER 3. Uprooted by her/his mother's death
And her/his baby brother's/sister's birth
The lass/lad forgot to tell the three
About the other sauna guest.

*(Music. **KING** enters and lies down.)*

STORYTELLER 1. It was a King who had been hunting
In the deep woods strayed and lost
He found the tupa and sought refuge.

STORYTELLER 2. Now he was in deepest slumber
So the three began to murmur
Like the birch leaves to each other.

SORCERESS 1. Let us say a charm so that the poor mother-less children may rest easy this night. Go forth, O pain!

SORCERESS 2. Fly on black wings over Tuonela's dark river

SORCERESS 3. to the Mountain of Misery.

SORCERESS 2. What kind of person do you think the new-born child will be when he/she grows up?

SORCERESS 3. Let us find out. Cast the bones. *(casts bones)*

ALL 3. A luck child!

STORYTELLER 2. At that moment, the King stirred from his sleep.

SORCERESS 1. Fortune declares that this boy/girl will become the heir of King Ahnas who is sleeping nearby.

(**KING** *hears this.*)

SORCERESS 1. When fortune declares a luck child, no matter how hard life may seem, fortunate he/she will be.

SORCERESS 3. Good night, good sisters.

OTHER SISTERS. Good night. (*They retire.*)

KING. (*rises*) So. Fortune links this wretched child to my fortune. May the sea swallow up these meddling sisters and spew their bones onto the rocky shore. I will see to the lucky child. (*lies back down*)

(*Music begins.*)

STORYTELLER 3. (*takes bucket to sisters*) In the morning the song birds sang.

(*Music cue.*)

STORYTELLER 1. The sisters three prepared to leave.

SORCERESS 1. (*washing from bucket*) Water of life.

SORCERESS 2. Water of healing. Water, the oldest of ointments.

SORCERESS 3. Let us be on our way without disturbing the motherless children and trust
That they are having a peaceful sleep.

(*They exit.*)

KING. (*arising, looking for sisters.*) Destiny is powerful, but I am more powerful. I must get that baby. (*calls out*) Helloooo.

LASS/LAD. (*entering with baby*) Good day to you, Your Majesty.

KING. Hyvää huomenta. Good day.

LASS/LAD. Forgive our humble home. Come in and have some bread with honey and a jug of fresh milk. I have just finished giving milk to the baby.

KING. I called not to trouble you, but to save you from trouble. You are poor and motherless and I am a king. I will pay you tuhat markkaa for this healthy babe and raise her/him as my heir. She/He will have the finest clothes, food and education and be of comfort to me in my old age.

LASS/LAD. Sell my brother/sister? I could as easily sell you the sun or the stars.

KING. If your poor departed mother were here she would tell you not to be so selfish. Think of the child and all he/she will gain in the bargain.

LASS/LAD. Ka, yes. I must think of his/her good. My heart must be silent so my head can hear.

KING. *(hands over a bag of gold)* Here is some gold to comfort you and your father when he returns. I will take good care of this wee one. *(takes baby)* Now. Where is the road?

LASS/LAD. Follow the birch trees to the clearing. You will see the road from there. Sweet brother/sister, I know you go to a sweeter life. *(music)* Here. Take this necklace from our dear mother to remind you always of our love.

*(**LASS/LAD** takes off a necklace and puts it on the baby, kisses baby, hands baby to **KING**, and exits.)*

KING. *(starts walking)* As soon as we are well out of sight, you wretched little crown stealer, I will leave you for the wolves and ravens. *(looking around)* Ah, my little would-be heir. *(throws the baby up like a ball and catches it)* An heir in the air. So much for good fortune. *(hides baby behind a bush)* Good riddance little weasel.

*(**KING** exits laughing. Music begins. **GOODY WOMAN** enters.)*

STORYTELLER 2. Soon a good woman wandered by
Searching the forest for food.

GOODY. Cloudberries. Mmmm....the first of the season. *(listens)* Hay month and bird cries everywhere. *(resumes berry picking, listens, searches)* No warbling thrushes here. Perhaps a squeaking wood mouse. *(She finds the baby.)* Heavens, a baby! Oh, you little clabber-mouthed woodchuck. Lost and alone in the dark woods. Brambles are not a proper bed. You'll go home with me to my humble tupa, you sweet little herring. I have cast a wish in each of the thousand lakes of Finland for a child. You are my wish come true. Come my little good berry. I will have you bearded with milk before you blink twice. *(She carries off the baby.)*

STORYTELLER 3. She called her sweet baby, Jukka/Liisa.
Tiny tumbler on her floor.

STORYTELLER 1. Pearl month, mud month turned the seasons.
The honeyed hills danced with bees.

STORYTELLER 2. Jukka/Liisa grew up strong and able
A gentle heart and full of cheer.

(Music begins.)

STORYTELLER 3. Till one day a storm raged over
Bringing the king to their door.

*(**KING** enters.)*

KING. Helloooo!

GOODY. *(entering, followed by* **JUKKA/LIISA***)* Who's there?

KING. *(shivering, shaking off water.)* Such a storm! I was out hunting and the power of the storm would not let me turn back and go home. It blew me to your door.

GOODY. Come inside and take refuge.

*(**KING** enters the house.)*

Child, fetch the traveller a warm drink.

*(**JUKKA/LIISA** exits to get something.)*

KING. A fine lad/lass indeed. And what is your son/daughter's name?

GOODY. Jukka/Liisa. Treasure of the forest. You see, I found him/her as a crying babe hidden among the brambles in the deep wild woods where I was gathering cloudberries. I brought him/her home and ever since, he/she has been the joy of my heart and household.

KING. *(growing suspicious)* And did this weas..uh baby have anything special about it? A mark? A note? A token?

(*JUKKA/LIISA enters.*)

GOODY. Yes indeed. A homespun cover, a hungry belly and a neck charm.

(*JUKKA/LIISA hands* KING *a cup and shows the necklace which was underneath shirt.*)

STORYTELLER 1. The king's hand began to tremble
And his heart began to rage
But he covered up his feelings.

KING. You are a healthy lad/lass. (*hands cup to* GOODY) I have an important message to be delivered to the palace. If you will take it, I will pay you well for your trouble.

JUKKA/LIISA. Ka, indeed. As you wish, Sire.

KING. (*writing*) Deliver this without delay to my wife, the queen.

JUKKA/LIISA. Yes, sire. Farewell dear mother. (*hugs her*) Without a horse, the journey is long. But I shall return before the peas grow fat in their pods.

GOODY. Safe journey, my son/daughter. Take both of the new-baked loaves by the hearth. And wrap yourself against the weather.

KING. (*aside*) A journey that will secure the safety of my fortune. (*to the* LAD/LASS) Speed you now. All haste is needed.

JUKKA/LIISA. It is good as done, sire.

(*JUKKA/LIISA exits.*)

KING. Well, the storm has passed. I take my leave of you, Goody. It has been time well spent. (*hands her a gold coin*) Here is something for your child's efforts.

GOODY. Thank you, sire.

(KING *leaves. Thunder.* GOODY *shivers.*)

What a dank chill follows the storm. No matter. Jukka/Liisa will soon be home.

(GOODY *exits.*)

(Music begins.)

STORYTELLER 2. Light of heart and nimble-footed
Through the hay woods he/she hurried
Until he/she met the sisters three.

(3 SORCERESSES *enter.)*

SORCERESSES. *(chanting and dancing)* Jukka/Liisa. Jukka/Liisa. Jukka/Liisa.

JUKKA/LIISA. You know my name?

SORCERESS 1. You heard your name?

JUKKA/LIISA. Ka.

SORCERESS 2. Perhaps it was the wind. The wind whispers to those who listen.

SORCERESS 3. And the saplings sing.

JUKKA/LIISA. Good sisters, I must go swiftly for I bear a message from the King.

SORCERESS 1. Yes, go swiftly. Swiftly to SLEEP.

(JUKKA/LIISA *is frozen.)*

SORCERESS 2. Deepest sleep.

SORCERESS 3. Your destiny to keep.

SORCERESS 1. Quickly, the letter.

(SORCERESS 2 *takes the letter from* **JUKKA/LIISA.***)*

SORCERESS 2. Just as we suspected. A message as black as the king's heart. "Kill the messenger who delivers this missive. He/she is our enemy."

SORCERESS 3. *(Casts a spell on the letter.)* As the seasons change from winter to spring, so the letter is changed from death to life.

SORCERESS 1. Out of the darkest times, something good will always come.

SORCERESSES. Wake now. Good fortune be yours.

(They exit.)

(Music begins.)

STORYTELLER 3. Jukka/Liisa delivered the letter to the Queen.

QUEEN. *(enters)* You have a letter for me?

JUKKA/LIISA. Yes, Your Majesty. *(kneels)*

QUEEN. *(reads from letter)* "Welcome this messenger as you would your own son/daughter. Take him/her into the palace and make him/her the heir to my fortune." I am most amazed! Your name, lad/lass?

JUKKA/LIISA. Jukka/Liisa, Your Majesty.

QUEEN. Well, Jukka/Liisa. You must have been the lucky one to find the almond in your rice pudding.

(extends hand to help JUKKA/LIISA *rise)*

Come. We will place sign and seal to the documents that will make you heir to this green gold kingdom.

JUKKA/LIISA. Now it is I who am most amazed.

QUEEN. Come and see your new home.

(They exit.)

STORYTELLER 1. Days later, when the King returned
He was in uproar and fury.

*(*QUEEN *enters with letter.* KING *follows.)*

QUEEN. It was all done as you specified in your letter. *(hands* KING *letter)*

KING. *(aside)* My sign. My seal. But not my words. Summon Jukka/Liisa immediately.

*(*QUEEN *leaves.)*

What is done cannot be undone. But I will send this usurper on a journey of no return.

*(*QUEEN *enters with* JUKKA/LIISA.*)*

Most fortunate youth, now that you are heir to my estate, you must prove that you are worthy of the honor. All my years, I have wondered what in life would bring the greatest happiness. The one who could answer that would be Louhi, Keeper of the Northland since she has traveled the world over.

QUEEN. But you might as well plunge serpent venom into this youth's heart. The journey to Louhi of the Northland is so long and arduous it is certain death.

KING. Don't be foolish. If this lad/lass has backbone, if he/
she has sisu, he/she will return. If not, he/she is not
worthy of being my heir.

JUKKA/LIISA. I am not afraid, Queen Mother. I will go
through granite if I must to prove my worthiness.
Farewell.

(**KING** *and* **QUEEN** *exit.* **JUKKA/LIISA** *begins the journey.*)

STORYTELLER 2. After days and days, Jukka/Liisa came
To the mountain top of Hiisi (*sound of wind begins*)
There swirled the Keeper of the Winds.

WIND. Music. Where are you going young traveler?

JUKKA/LIISA. Who are you?

WIND. I am Keeper of the Eight Winds of the World.

JUKKA/LIISA. I am bound for the far Northland to ask
Louhi what in life brings the greatest happiness.

WIND. I also have a question for Louhi. If you will ask
Louhi for me, I will blow you to the Northland.

JUKKA/LIISA. Ka. I will ask your question.

WIND. I have an orchard that used to bear fine fruit. Now,
before the fruit can ripen, it is full of fuzz mold. Ask
Louhi what I can do about it.

JUKKA/LIISA. That I will.

WIND. North wind blow and north wind furl
Sweep this youth into your swirl.
Take him/her up to your home
To Mount Misery's highest dome.

(*Wind sounds swell as* **KEEPER** *of the Wind whirls off.*)

STORYTELLER 3. The wind blew Jukka/Liisa to the North
Setting him/her down at a troll cave.

(*Wind sound subsides as cave drip/echo is heard.*)
The angry troll was struggling
With a box that would not open.

(**TROLL** *enters and tries to open box.*)

TROLL. Why won't this key work? *(anger mounts)* Moose muffins! What's the matter with it? *(turns key this way and that)* Someone has witched the lock shut. A pox on them. May they be struck with colic, gout, itch and plague*!* (**TROLL** *pounds on the box, kicks the box, stubs toe, and yelps.)*

JUKKA/LIISA. *(taken aback)* Begging your pardon.

TROLL. I'll pardon your begging if you get this box open.

(**JUKKA/LIISA** *tries.)*

Onions and bunions. The world is full of tears and misery. Can't a body go about the business of the day without the good parts being gnawed into one big canker? Is it too much to ask for milk not spoiled with curdle, bones without ache and a key to turn in a lock? What kind of excuse do you have for meddling in my affairs you yap-mouthed upstart?

JUKKA/LIISA. I'm searching for Louhi to find the answer to what in life brings happiness.

TROLL. Happiness? Is that your question?

(**JUKKA/LIISA** *nods.)*

Happiness is like a wart. It comes and goes as it pleases. But a key to a chest full of treasure. Now that is a pike with a different stripe. You ask Louhi how to make this key work and I'll give you treasures from inside.

JUKKA/LIISA. Ka. Indeed I will.

TROLL. Go straight until you get to a wide black river. You must cross to the other side to find Louhi.

JUKKA/LIISA. Thank you.

TROLL. Don't forget to ask about my key.

JUKKA/LIISA. I won't.

(**TROLL** *exits. Cave sounds subside as the sound of a flowing river begins)*

STORYTELLER 1. He/she journeyed to the river black
Where he/she met the rower of the boat.

(**RIVER ROWER** *enters carrying an oar.)*

JUKKA/LIISA. Good rower of the river. I need to cross to the other side.

RIVER ROWER. For many years I've been ferrying people across this black river and no one has ever relieved me. Will you take the oar so I can stop rowing?

JUKKA/LIISA. Regretfully no. I am on my way to ask Louhi the answer to what in life brings happiness.

RIVER ROWER. Here I am, back and forth, forth and back across this black river. And I have nothing but a handful of blisters and fungus feet to show for my life. Others come and go on their way to other places, other sights, other sounds. But not me. I'm left behind. You ask Louhi why I must forever be ferrying people across this river. I'm weary of it. Weary to the bones. Weary to the soles of my soggy feet. Promise to ask Louhi and I'll row you across.

JUKKA. Ka. I will. *(mimes getting in boat)*

RIVER ROWER. You hear the oars creaking? They are forever repeating, "shore to shore, nothing more. Shore to shore, nothing more." Remember to ask Louhi my question.

JUKKA/LIISA. I promise. *(waves farewell)*

RIVER ROWER. Go that way until you come to a fork in the road. There is a smooth path and a bramble path. Follow the bramble path to the end.

JUKKA/LIISA. Thank you. I will.

(**RIVER ROWER** *exits as water sound subsides. Music begins.*)

STORYTELLER 2. Through the tangles of prickly thorns
Jukka/Liisa trod to the house of Louhi.
There he/she called until the door opened.

JUKKA/LIISA. Hallo. Halloooo.

(**AURORA** *enters.*)

STORYTELLER 3. Out came shimmering northern lights,
Rainbow Aurora Borealis.

AURORA. Hyvää huomenta. Hello.

JUKKA. Hyvää huomenta. My name is Jukka/Liisa.

AURORA. And I am called Aurora.

JUKKA/LIISA. May I ask a few questions of Louhi?

AURORA. My mother is not here. But I expect her by nightfall.

JUKKA/LIISA. I have traveled far to ask her. Please, may I wait until she returns?

AURORA. You have an honest face and a kind smile…so yes. You can wait. I'm curious, though. What are your questions. Perhaps I could shed a glimmer of light.

STORYTELLER 1. Jukka/Liisa told her all his questions Aurora's silver laughter rang.

AURORA. *(laughing)* You don't want to know much, do you? I fear my mother will not answer all your questions. She has little patience with human foolishness.

*(**JUKKA/LIISA** looks dejected.)*

Oh, don't look so sad. I have an idea. You must hide yourself and I will ask the questions for you. Listen carefully to Louhi's answers and when the washed out moon disappears, you can slip out and she will be none the wiser.

JUKKA. How can I ever thank you for your kindness?

(Icicle music begins.)

AURORA. I hear her coming. Hide quickly.

*(**JUKKA/LIISA** hides.)*

LOUHI. *(enters)* Hyvää iltaa, daughter.

AURORA. Hyvää iltaa, mother.

LOUHI. Has anyone come while I was gone?

AURORA. A lad/lass came this morning full of questions. But you were not home so I sent the youth away to ask elsewhere.

LOUHI. What a pity. Most humans have no more sense than the turnips they eat. I could have answered anything he/she wanted to know.

AURORA. I know, mother. The North Wind sweeps all knowledge to your feet.

LOUHI. What sort of questions did the youth ask?

AURORA. First he/she wanted to know what in life brings happiness?

LOUHI. Humans, humans, humans. Always searching for happiness. Seeking happiness is like trying to catch the flicker of your dancing lights, Aurora. Don't they listen to their own sayings? "People are happiest when they plow their fields, clear the soil and plant seeds that will grow for themselves and their animals." Turnips! Turnips have more sense. What else did this youth want to know?

AURORA. He/she asked why the orchard of the Keeper of the Eight Winds bears fruit that is full of fuzz mold.

LOUHI. Simple! Find the worm in the garden. There you find the rot. What else?

AURORA. There was a troll who wanted to know how to get the key to turn the lock.

LOUHI. Locks! Keys! That which is of value should not be hidden away. The troll should know that no key is needed. Just lift the lid and the treasure will be revealed without struggle. Anything else?

AURORA. One more question. The River Rower who ferries the boat across the black river want to know how to escape his/her bondage?

LOUHI. When the Rower ferries someone across, all he/she has to do is jump ashore and push the boat off with his/her heel. Then the passenger will have to row the boat until someone new comes along and they can do the same thing. If anyone comes asking questions again, mind you, don't tell them the answers. I don't know why, but simple-minded questions like these are considered mysterious secrets to humans. If you have a hole in your thinking, what can you expect but a leaky boat. Come. Let's go sit down to supper.

(*LOUHI* exits. *AURORA* waves to *JUKKA/LIISA* who mouths *"thank you." **AURORA** exits. Music begins.*)

(**RIVER ROWER** *enters.*)

STORYTELLER 2. When Jukka/Liisa came back to the shore, The River Rower queried him/her.

RIVER ROWER. What did Louhi say in answer to my question?

JUKKA/LIISA. I'll tell you as soon as you set me ashore on the other side.

RIVER ROWER. Once more, the oars say

Shore to shore, nothing more.

Tell me now, lad/lass.

JUKKA/LIISA. This is Louhi's answer. With your heel, shove the next traveler off the shore in your boat and then get on with the rest of your life. The traveler will then have to ferry your boat until someone new comes along.

RIVER ROWER. Why didn't I think of that? Thank you lad/lass. Thank you. (*Exits.*)

JUKKA/LIISA. Now, straight away to the troll cave.

(**TROLL** *enters.*)

Good day.

TROLL. What's good about it, you over-perky pest. Did you find out the answer to my question?

JUKKA/LIISA. Indeed. You don't need a key. Just lift the lid of your box.

TROLL. Make fun of me will you? (*puts down key and tries opening the box*) I'll roast you till your tongue is wagging a different (*box opens*) ...It opened!. Son of a woodchuck! Look, look! My treasure! What a wonderful lad/lass you are. (*rifling through treasure*) Wonderful, wonderful. A veritable genius you are. Here. Have a necklace. Have two. Stuff your pockets with gold.

JUKKA/LIISA. Thank you. This is more than enough.

TROLL. No keys! No locks! How simple. How lovely. (*exits dancing a bobbity little dance and singing*) No keys, no locks. No keys, no locks...

JUKKA/LIISA. Catch a wind back to Mount Hissi.

(Music. **WIND KEEPER** *swirls in.)*

WIND. Do you have an answer from Louhi for me?

JUKKA. Yes, I do. Louhi says, "find the worm, find the rot."

WIND. Find the worm, find the rot? Amazing. Such a small answer to such a big problem. Thank you. Now, how can I help you?

JUKKA/LIISA. Will you please blow me back to the palace?

WIND. Of course. South Wind blow and South Wind furl. Sweep this lad/lass into your swirl.

(Spins off. Music begins.)

JUKKA/LIISA. Off to the palace.

*(***KING*** and ***QUEEN*** *enter.)*

QUEEN. Jukka/Liisa, dear lad/lass. You are safe. How glad I am to see you.

KING. *(furious)* Imposter! You can't have been to Louhi of the Northland and back again so soon.

JUKKA/LIISA. But, Sire, I have. And in answer to your question, Louhi says "People are happiest when they plow their fields, clear the soil, and plant seeds that will grow for themselves and their animals."

KING. What kind of answer is that? I'm a king, not a farmer.

QUEEN. Of course you are, dear. I'm sure Louhi wasn't just referring to growing vegetables, but to good work of all manner: planting seeds of care and kindness and…

KING. Gold! Where did you get all this gold?

STORYTELLER 3. Jukka/Liisa told about his/her adventure.

KING. Where'd you say that troll cave was?

*(***JUKKA/LIISA*** *points.)*

And the River Rower who ferried you across the black river to Louhi?

*(***JUKKA/LIISA*** *points again.)*

I'm off. For I have a thing or two to ask Louhi myself.

*(***KING*** *exits. Music. Remaining cast enters.)*

LOUHI. Straightway, the King set off alone
    And has not been seen since then.

AURORA. Now the River Rower's boat
    The King must ferry evermore.

RIVER ROWER. Throughout Finland, this tale's been told
    Of Jukka's/Liisa's wondrous adventure.

TROLL. To find the answer for the King
    Of what in life brings happiness.

STORYTELLER 1. Now the Finns embrace each season.

WIND. Welcome each for all it brings

JUKKA/LIISA. Mounding pristine snows of pearl month

LASS/LAD. Melt into mud month's wet slush.

GOODY. First-picked strawberries bring great joy.
    Then comes hay month's golden harvest.

QUEEN. The King's great wealth and all the land
    Were Jukka's/Liisa's now to wisely rule.

SORCERESSES. As was foretold when he/she was born.

STORYTELLER 1. All you who listen to this tale

STORYTELLER 2. Knit from frost who sang its verses

STORYTELLER 3. Knit from rhyme the rain recited

STORYTELLER 1. Knit from tales the wind delivered
    All those who listen know full well

ALL. The sea and fortune will prevail.

(music and curtain)

PRODUCTION NOTES

The Kalevala is the national epic poem of Finland. During the nineteenth century, *The Kalevala* was compiled by the folklorist, Elias Lonnrot, in the course of twelve trips made on foot or skis to the vast regions in and around Finland. Lonnrot collected the songs and poems from oral tradition and wove them into a long narrative poem. Immediately, *The Kalevala* helped to create a sense of national identity. Jean Sibelius's symphony, Finlandia, was inspired by *The Kalevala* and is the main source for musical cues in *Song of the Sea.*

Hyvää iltaa – *(Hue-va ill-ta)* Good evening.

Hyvää huomenta — *(Hue-va hoe-a-menta)* Good day.

Kiitos – *(kee-tus)* Thank you

Tupa – *(too-pa)* Farm house

Many of the roles are flex-gendered, as indicated. Some of the other roles (Storytellers, Troll and Wind) can be flex-gendered, as well. The number of Storytellers can be adapted to more or less Storytellers as needed, as can the roles of the Troll and the Sorceresses.

TOPICS FOR DISCUSSION

Fate/destiny vs. free will.

In what ways is the journey of Jukka/Liisa similar or different to our own journey?

In modern times, who might be the counterparts to each of the characters in the play?

What are the embedded metaphors in Louhi's answer to the question, "what in life brings happiness?"

THE HAND OF FRIENDSHIP

A folk tale from India

The Hand of Friendship was first presented by Metastages Theatre Centre on April 24, 1999 at the Paul Robeson Cultural Center, Penn State University, University Park, Pennsylvania. The cultural advisor was Dr. Indu Mulay. The production was directed by the author and included the following cast:

SHANTA . . . . Kathryn Supina

INDU . . . . Alyssa Drobka

RAVI . . . . Rachel Thor

OSAMA . . . . Megan Supina

SONALI . . . . Clara Arnold

TEACHER JAHAN . . . . Sarah Tiberio Shultz

PIPAL TREE . . . . Christina Carpenter

WATER BUFFALO . . . . Luba Guzei

ELEPHANT . . . . Molly Ryan

BRAHMAN 1 . . . . Samantha Bernecker

BRAHMAN 2 . . . . Christopher Ryves

BRAHMAN 3 . . . . Kristen Granger

TAJ TIGER . . . . Steven Tippeconnic

KHAN TIGER . . . . Katie Gill

JACKAL 1 . . . . Stevie Moore

JACKAL 2 . . . . Lauren Robertson

CHARACTERS

SHANTA, the dancing teacher
INDU, a student
RAVI, a student
OSAMA, a student
SONALI, a student
JAHAN, the acting teacher
MIRA, the pipal tree
PUNJAB, the elephant
NANDA, the water buffalo
BRAHMAN 1
BRAHMAN 2
BRAHMAN 3
JACKAL 1
JACKAL 2
TAJ, a tiger
KHAN, a tiger

*(Sitar Music. **SHANTA**, the teacher, dances on followed by four students, **INDU**, **RAVI**, **OSAMA** and **SONALI**. Students imitate the moves of **SHANTA** who mimes the elements of air, water, fire and earth. As the dance concludes, the teacher and students bow respectfully to each other. Then the students collapse on the ground, groaning and nursing various sore spots.)*

SHANTA. Very good. Very good. You become better and better with each practice.

INDU. But, Teacher, why must we spend our afternoons dancing while our friends play?

RAVI. Yes, it's not fair!

OSAMA. All we do is work work work.

SONALI. *(groaning)* I can hardly move my muscles.

SHANTA. In India, all things have a purpose. Your purpose, students, is to create beauty through the art of dancing.

RAVI. Why us?

OSAMA. Why can't someone else do the dancing?

SHANTA. Because you have been given the *talent* to be dancers.

INDU. What's so special about that?

SONALI. We just want to be like everyone else.

SHANTA. Never wish away your talent. It is what gives you purpose in life.

*(Enter **JAHAN**, the acting teacher, in a state of concern.)*

JAHAN. Namaste, my friends. *(pronounced: nah-mah-stay, meaning "hello")*

SHANTA. Look, students, it is Jahan, the acting teacher.

STUDENTS. Namaste, Teacher.

JAHAN. Good day, students. Teacher Shanta, I have a problem and I need your help. My acting students have rehearsed a play, but they have no audience to perform it for.

SHANTA. And how could I help?

JAHAN. Would you be so kind as to suspend your dance practice long enough for us to perform the play?

INDU. Oh, please, Teacher Shanta! We want to see the play.

RAVI. We promise to practice without complaining if you let us.

JAHAN. It's quite short, and without an audience, the actors have no purpose.

OSAMA. Let us help them, please!

SONALI. We can be their purpose!

SHANTA. Very well, let us see and hear this play.

JAHAN. Oh, thank you, Teacher Shanta! *(claps hands and calls)*

Company, take your places! We have found an audience at last!

*(Actors troup on making last minute adjustment to their costumes and masks. A large cage is rolled on. **MIRA**, an actor dressed as a pipal tree, takes a position. As they prepare, the dancing students comment.)*

SONALI. Look! Is that a tree?

INDU. It looks like a tree.

RAVI. Of course it's a tree.

MIRA. Yes, I'm a tree. A pipal You can tell by my leaves.

SONALI. *(seeing* **WATER BUFFALO***)* What a funny cow!

OSAMA. Look at its horns!

RAVI. Silly! That is no cow. It's a buffalo.

NANDA. You are right. I'm a buffalo. A water buffalo.

INDU. *(as* **ELEPHANT** *passes* **WATER BUFFALO***)* And an elephant! Or do you think it's another cow, Sonali?

PUNJAB. Everyone knows what an elephant looks like.

SONALI. *(as* **BRAHMANS** *enter)* This time I know. Those are Brahmans. Poor Brahmans.

SHANTA. And what is the purpose of a Brahman?

INDU. Brahmans help all things great and small.

OSAMA. They have good hearts, but do not always use the best sense.

RAVI. *(as* **JACKALS** *cross)* And there are the jackals, the clever young jackals.

JAHAN. You will soon find out how clever they are.

OSAMA. Two Bengal tigers, the fiercest of beasts! They are trapped in a cage.

JAHAN. *(announces)* And now our story begins!

(The **TIGERS** *begin wailing in anguish. They are crying for help.)*

BRAHMAN 1. Oh, look! Those poor tigers.

BRAHMAN 2. They are unhappy to be held against their will.

TAJ TIGER. Oh, Brahmans! Sweet Brahmans!

BRAHMAN 3. Do not flatter us.

KHAN TIGER. Dear, good, sweet, wise, Brahmans. Please let us out of this cage.

BRAHMAN 1. Why should we trust you?

BRAHMAN 2. Your teeth are long and sharp.

BRAHMAN 3. And you look quite hungry.

TAJ TIGER. Kind Brahmans. Please let us out. If you don't, we shall be killed and skinned for some rich man's rug!

BRAHMAN 1. And if we free you, we may very well become your dinner.

KHAN TIGER. How can you say such things. Let us out and we shall repay your kindness with gratitude.

BRAHMAN 2. I wish we could believe you. But, no. Your claws are too long.

TAJ TIGER. We use them only to protect ourselves. Never to harm friends.

BRAHMAN 3. Do you really mean that? If we let you out, you would not harm us?

KHAN TIGER. Sweet Brahmans, we promise to cherish and protect you always.

(**BRAHMANS** *cautiously open the cage door. Immediately the* **TIGERS** *growl, pounce on them and pin them to the ground.*)

STUDENTS. Oh, no!

TAJ TIGER. Fools! You stupid Brahmans!

KHAN TIGER. You should have more sense.

BRAHMAN 1. Oh, tigers, have mercy!

BRAHMAN 2. Remember your promise!

TAJ TIGER. Pooh! What's a promise to a tiger! You will make a tasty dinner.

KHAN TIGER. A bit thin, but tender I suspect.

BRAHMAN 3. Is this how you show your gratitude?

TAJ TIGER. Always remember, Brahmans, a tiger never lets its dinner walk away.

BRAHMAN 1. Our end is here!

BRAHMAN 2. Do not eat us, I beg of you. Give us another chance. We saved your life. Now spare ours.

KHAN TIGER. (*looks at* **TAJ TIGER**, *then back to the* **BRAHMANS**) Very well. We will prove to you how foolish you are. Go and ask the first three things you meet what we should do with you. We will follow their advice. If even one of them agrees that we have been unfair, we will let you go.

TAJ TIGER. Now be gone, stupid fools. You will soon be back for our dinner.

(**TIGERS** *stroll behind the cage as the* **BRAHMANS** *look around for help.*)

BRAHMAN 3. Surely the village sees how unfair the tigers have been to us.

INDU. Oh look, there's the pipal tree.

BRAHMAN 1. *(approaches the tree)* Perhaps this pipal tree will help. Namaste, beautiful Tree. Will you hear our story?

PIPAL TREE. Speak, Brahmans. I am listening.

BRAHMAN 1. Two savage tigers were caught in a cage. They promised to show gratitude if we let them out.

BRAHMAN 2. But when we freed them, they attacked us and threatened to eat us.

BRAHMAN 3. Do you think they treated us fairly?

PIPAL TREE. As fair as I am ever treated.

BRAHMAN 1. What do you mean, Pipal Tree?

PIPAL TREE. I stand here day and night providing shade and shelter for people. Even on the very hottest of days I keep my branches spread to protect travelers from the sun's scorching rays.

BRAHMAN 2. Indeed you do. I, myself, have often sat and read under your cooling boughs.

PIPAL TREE. But does anyone ever give me even a drop of water in return? No! Instead they tear off my branches and feed them to their cattle. The tigers have treated you as fairly as people treat me. I do not wish you ill, but you are getting what you deserve.

BRAHMAN 3. Oh, no!

PIPAL TREE. Don't look for any pity from me. Good bye.
    (**PIPAL TREE** *turns away.*)

RAVI. Poor tree.

OSAMA. Poor Brahmans!

SONALI. There is the elephant.

BRAHMAN 1. How unexpected. But we still have two more chances.

(*Sees* **PUNJAB THE ELEPHANT** *chained to a log.*)

Surely this elephant will help us!

(*The* **BRAHMANS** *approach the* **ELEPHANT**.)

BRAHMAN 2. Namaste, friend Elephant. Please listen to our plight.

ELEPHANT. Listen? What else can I do? I am chained to this place and cannot move. What is it you have to say?

BRAHMAN 3. Two Bengal tigers promised to cherish and protect us if we released them from a cage. But when we did, they pounced on us and threatened to eat us.

ELEPHANT. *(sarcastically)* What else would you expect of tigers?

BRAHMAN 1. Surely you don't find their behavior to be just.

ELEPHANT. Just? Don't talk to me about justice. Since I was a calf, my owner has kept me captive with this chain around my leg. When he rides me, he beats me with a rod so I will go faster. I have never known a moment's freedom. Tell me, do you think there is any justice in my life?

BRAHMAN 2. But it is our duty to obey the orders of our master.

ELEPHANT. Then obey the tigers and let them eat you! I wish you luck, but don't expect me to feel sorry for you.

BRAHMANS. But... .

ELEPHANT. You should never have freed wild tigers in the first place. Good day! (**ELEPHANT** *turns away.*)

BRAHMAN 3. Alas! We have just one more chance. Is there no end to our troubles?

(**WATER BUFFALO** *comes lumbering by slowly.*)

BRAHMAN 1. There's an old water buffalo. Surely it will help us.

WATER BUFFALO. *(passing)* Namaste, Brahmans.

BRAHMAN 2. Honest Water Buffalo, please hear our story!

WATER BUFFALO. Very well. I will listen. But you had better make it fast. I haven't much time left for this world.

BRAHMAN 3. Oh, revered Water Buffalo, you will pity us when you hear our dilemma.

BRAHMAN 1. In an act of friendship, we released two ferocious tigers from a cage once they promised not to harm us. Immediately they announced they would eat us for dinner!

BRAHMAN 2. Was this behavior fair?

WATER BUFFALO. Well, you are fools to expect gratitude! You will know why I say this when you hear my story. When I was young and gave milk, my owners fed me tender grains and fragrant pipal leaves. But now that I am old and dry, they throw me slop and trash. Even the pigs refuse the food that I am supposed to eat. No one offers to help me. Do you call that fair?

BRAHMAN 3. Of course not.

WATER BUFFALO. But it is the way of the world. I feel no pity for you, fools. You get what you deserve. Good day.

(**WATER BUFFALO** *leaves.*)

STUDENTS. Oh no!

BRAHMAN 1. That was our last chance! No one agrees with us.

BRAHMAN 2. There is no hope for us. We must return to the tigers.

(*As they approach the empty tiger cage with downcast eyes, the* **JACKALS** *enters and see them.*)

JACKAL 1. Namaste, good Brahmans! What makes you so sad?

BRAHMAN 3. Ah, Jackal, we must say good-bye forever.

BRAHMAN 1. We are about to be eaten by the very tigers we freed.

JACKAL 2. Tigers?

BRAHMAN 2. It's a long story.

BRAHMAN 3. We're only getting what we deserve.

(*As the* **BRAHMANS** *approach the cage, the* **TIGERS** *emerge to greet them.*)

TAJ TIGER. Welcome back, fools, we expected you sooner.

KHAN TIGER. Yes, it's past our dinner time. We're starving.

JACKAL 1. Wait! Wait! I don't understand this story! (*to the dancing students who are watching the play*) Someone tell me what has happened.

INDU. You see, the two Bengal tigers were trapped in the cage.

OSAMA. And the Brahmans came walking by.

JACKAL 2. Dear me, what were the Brahmans doing in a tiger cage?

RAVI. No, the tigers were in the cage.

SONALI. And the Brahmans were walking by.

JACKAL 1. Oh, my poor head. My poor head. I'm getting dizzy. *(to dancing students)* You were all dancing in a tiger cage?

TAJ TIGER. Fool! *We* were in the cage!

JACKAL 2. *(to TAJ TIGER)* The same cage I was in?

KHAN TIGER. You weren't in the cage, stupid. *We* were in the cage!

JACKAL 1. I must take this slowly. My poor head is spinning. Let me see. *(to students, looking for confirmation)* The Brahmans were in the cage, right?

STUDENTS. No!

JACKAL 2. I mean, I was a tiger and the cage came walking by...

STUDENTS. Noooo!

JACKAL 1. The cage was eating the tigers for dinner, and...

STUDENTS & TIGERS. Nooooooo!

KHAN TIGER. *(stepping in)* See here! I am a tiger! Do you understand that?

JACKAL 2. You are a tiger. Yes, yes, of course.

TAJ TIGER. And those are the Brahmans. Do you understand that?

JACKAL 1. Yes...I think so. *(pointing)* They are Brahmans.

KHAN TIGER. And this is the cage. Do you understand that?

JACKAL 2. Um...I...ummn...I'm pretty clear...but not quite.

TAJ TIGER. *(frustrated)* What don't you understand?

KHAN TIGER. *(shouting)* What is not clear?

JACKAL 1. Well, there is one small detail.

KHAN TIGER. Hurry up! We're at the end of our patience!

JACKAL 2. Please, oh great ones. *(pause)* How did you get in the cage?

TAJ TIGER. How did we get in? Is your head filled with buffalo dung? Everyone knows how we got in!

JACKAL 1. And how is that?

TAJ TIGER. This way, of course. *(to* **KHAN***)* Come, show the fool!

(Both **TIGERS** *jump into the cage.)*

KHAN TIGER. *(inside the cage)* Now do you understand?

JACKALS: Of course! *(quickly closing and latching the cage door)*

JACKAL 2. And if it's all the same to you, we'll let you stay right where you are!

JACKAL 1. *(turning to* **BRAHMANS***)* As for you, friends, you must learn to understand the true nature of all things both great and small.

(music)

(Dance students, led by **SHANTA** *and* **JAHAN***, applaud vigorously as the actors line up before them and bow. Then all celebrate in dance.)*

(curtain)

TOPICS FOR DISCUSSION

Can you think of a situation where someone experienced consequences because of the "true nature" of something?

Is it possible for life to be fair all the time?

THE PRIDEFUL PRINCESS

**A Folktale from the Ashanti People
of Ghana – West Africa**

THE PRIDEFUL PRINCESS was first presented by the MetaStages Theatre Centre on April 15, 2000 at the Pavilion Theatre, Penn State University, University Park, PA. The cultural advisor was Dr. Clemente Abrokwa. The production was directed by the author and featured the following cast:

GRIOT KOUMBA . . . . Brianna Faust

GRIOT ASHAKI . . . . Ethan Pierick

GRIOT OKOLO . . . . Robbin Zirkle

QUEEN. . . . . Jasmine Silver

ADVISOR . . . . .Kevin Ford

PRINCESS . . . . .Medha Raj

HANDMAIDEN 1 . . . . .Sarah Hall

HANDMAIDEN 2 . . . . Katherine Bailey

BIRD 1 . . . . Lauren Schloss

BIRD 2 . . . . Breanna Gibson

BEGGAR CHILD 1 . . . . Leah Mueller

BEGGAR CHILD 2 . . . . .Emma Cusumano

PRINCESS FUTI/FLOWER. . . . . .Alexandra Goetz

DOCTOR/MOUSE. . . . . Jason Rapisarda

ANT 1/COURTIER 1 . . . . .Ricky Stoekl

ANT 2/COURTIER 2 . . . . .Nicholas Field

CHARACTERS

GRIOT KOUMBA
GRIOT ASHAKI
GRIOT OKOLO
QUEEN
ADVISOR
PRINCESS
HANDMAIDEN 1
HANDMAIDEN 2
BIRD 1
BIRD 2
BEGGAR CHILD 1
BEGGAR CHILD 2
PRINCESS FUTI/FLOWER
DOCTOR/MOUSE
ANT 1/COURTIER 1
ANT 2/COURTIER 2

(All enter singing and dancing. **GRIOTS** *address the audience.)*

GRIOT KOUMBA. Our lives depend upon the land.

GRIOT ASHAKI. So, when the rains don't come the crops suffer.

GRIOT OKOLO. The animals suffer.

ALL GRIOTS. The people suffer.

GRIOT KOUMBA. Here is a story to remind us that even the smallest ant can make the world a better place.

GRIOT ASHAKI. The story of a prideful princess.

GRIOT OKOLO. One morning the village queen arose early.

*(***QUEEN*** enters with ***ADVISOR.****)*

QUEEN. A most beautiful day, Advisor. The sun is up. Is my daughter about?

ADVISOR. Yes, Majesty. Her handmaidens are weaving golden braid into the hair of the Princess at this very moment. Ah, here they come.

*(Enter ***PRINCESS*** with two ***HANDMAIDENS*** carrying the long train of her hair.)*

QUEEN. Wo ho te sen. Good morning, daughter. Daughter, your hair is longer than it was yesterday.

PRINCESS. I know. *(aloof)* People always admire my beautiful hair.

QUEEN. Don't be so prideful, dear. All people have a gift that makes them beautiful.

*(***QUEEN*** exits with ***ADVISOR.****)*

HANDMAIDEN 1. *(to ***HANDMAIDEN*** 2)* Be careful there. Her hair is like satin. Don't let it slip.

HANDMAIDEN 2. I won't. I have a tight grip.

PRINCESS. Oww. You are pulling my hair.

HANDMAIDEN 2. Ohhh, sorry. I'm so sorry, Princess.

PRINCESS. Don't let it happen again.

HANDMAIDEN 2. No no, Your Highness. I won't.

HANDMAIDEN 1. Would you like to sit here in the garden? It's a beautiful morning.

PRINCESS. Yes. But be careful. *(They sit.)*

GRIOT KOUMBA. As the Princess and her handmaidens settled, two birds flew into the garden.

 *(**BIRDS** enter.)*

HANDMAIDEN 2. Oh look. Two birds from the Kava forest.

BIRD 1. Wo ho te sen. Good morning, Princess.

BIRD 2. We've heard so much about your hair that we had to come and see for ourselves.

BIRD 1. It's even more beautiful than I could have imagined.

BIRD 2. Perhaps you could spare a few strands so that we may weave them into our nests?

PRINCESS. My magnificent hair for a bird's nest? How dare you!

BIRD 1. Just a little.

BIRD 2. You wouldn't even miss it.

PRINCESS. Go away.

BIRD 1. Is that your final word?

HANDMAIDEN 1. Princess, shall I call the guard?

BIRD 2. That won't be necessary. We'll leave.

BIRD 1. But one day you will wish you had been kinder.

BIRD 2. When the dry season comes, beware. For when the leaves fall,

BOTH BIRDS. so shall your hair.

 *(**PRINCESS** and **MAIDENS** gasp.)*

HANDMAIDEN 2. Don't pay any attention, Princess. They are just foolish birds.

HANDMAIDEN 1. Yes jealous, foolish birds.

 *(**HANDMAIDENS** and **PRINCESS** exit.)*

GRIOT ASHAKI. As the birds continued to search for soft linings for their nests, two beggar children came by.

(**BEGGARS 1 & 2** *enter. They see the* **BIRDS**.)

BEGGAR 1. Ohhh, those birds.

BEGGAR 2. Ohhh, those birds what?

BEGGAR 1. Those birds would make a fine meal.

BEGGAR 2. Yes. One for each of us. Oh, I'm so hungry.

(**BIRDS** *fly off.*)

BEGGAR 1. I think I have some berries left. (*reaches in kinja*) Hmmm…only two.

BEGGAR 2. (*laughs*) One for each of us. Let's take a nap. Maybe our stomachs will forget about food.

(*Other nods in agreement. They settle down to sleep.*)

GRIOT OKOLO. As the beggar children slept, they dreamt of the birds. (*sound of chirping*)

GRIOT KOUMBA. In their dreams they had a bow and arrow, but the birds flew off before they could shoot.

GRIOT ASHAKI. The birds disappeared along a lonely path over the plains into a deep red sunset.

GRIOT OKOLO. Each time the beggars went to sleep, they had the same dream.

GRIOT KOUMBA. Months passed and a terrible drought was upon the land. (*sounds of wind*)
The rivers dried up. Huge cracks opened like gaping mouths in the earth.

GRIOT ASHAKI. The crops withered. The leaves crumbled and fell from the trees. A fierce wind savaged the land. (*more wind*)

GRIOT OKOLO. One day, the Princess was walking with her handmaidens who were tending her hair.

(**PRINCESS** *and* **HANDMAIDENS** *enter.*)

HANDMAIDEN 1. It's time for your best friend, Princess Futi, to visit.

HANDMAIDEN 2. Here she comes now.

(**PRINCESS FUTI** *enters. She is very aloof.*)

PRINCESS FUTI. Wo ho te sen. Good day.

PRINCESS. Wo ho te sen, Princess Futi.

PRINCESS FUTI. I'm so glad that you will be coming to my party tomorrow. Everybody who is anybody will be there.

PRINCESS. Oh yes, I would not miss it. (*stronger wind sounds*)

HANDMAIDEN 1. The wind howls so.

HANDMAIDEN 2. (*all cough*) Dust. Dust. Clouds of dust.

(*A huge cloud of dust churns by and blows the* **PRINCESS**'s *hair away.* **HANDMAIDENS** *and* **PRINCESS FUTI** *gasp at her bald head.*)

PRINCESS FUTI. (*horrified*) About the party…uhhh…I know you have much bigger problems to worry about, Princess. So, don't bother to come. It wouldn't look right. You understand, I'm sure. (*runs off*)

PRINCESS. (*puzzled*) Understand what?

HANDMAIDEN 1. Your hair!

PRINCESS. What? Did the wind mess it up? (*puts hands up to head and gasps*) My hair! Where's my hair!

HANDMAIDEN 2. The wind blew it away.

PRINCESS. All of it?

HANDMAIDENS. All of it!

(**PRINCESS** *feels head and screams then runs off shrieking followed by* **HANDMAIDENS.**)

GRIOT KOUMBA. The Queen learned of the Princess's dilemma and summoned the court advisor.

(*Enter* **ADVISOR, QUEEN,** *and* **COURTIER 1.**)

QUEEN. What can we do to restore the Princess's hair? She stays in her room day and night.

ADVISOR. (*to* **COURTIER 1**) Courtier, go and get the Princess.

COURTIER 1. As you wish. (*exits*)

ADVISOR. I have sent for the court doctor. Here he/she comes now.

(Enter **DOCTOR** *led by* **COURTIER 2**. *)*

COURTIER 2. *(announces)* The doctor of the court.

QUEEN. Thank you, Courtier.

(waves **COURTIER** *aside)*

DOCTOR. *(bows)* Your Majesty.

QUEEN. You are aware of the problem?

DOCTOR. Yes. The advisor has briefed me.

(Enter **PRINCESS, MAIDENS** *and* **COURTIER.** *)*

Ah, Your Highness....

(begins to examine **PRINCESS** *)*

Hmmm..... hmmmm...

QUEEN. Well? What can we do?

DOCTOR. Perhaps a mixture of beetle dung and pulverized yam.

(takes some from bag and begins to massage it into the **PRINCESS** *'s scalp)*

PRINCESS. Ewwwww!!!!

(looks at **HANDMAIDENS** *and they respond sympathetically)*

DOCTOR. Rub it into the scalp daily to encourage new growth.

(hands salve to **PRINCESS** *)*

ADVISOR. How long will that take?

DOCTOR. This is a very puzzling case.

QUEEN. Two weeks? A month ? Two months?

DOCTOR. Since the cause for the hair loss is unknown, the cure is equally uncertain. *(bows)*

ADVISOR. That is unacceptable, Doctor.

(waves to **COURTIERS 1 & 2** *who lead* **DOCTOR** *off)*

GRIOT ASHAKI. Weeks passed, but the only thing that grew was a distinctly unpleasant smell coming from the head of the Princess.

QUEEN. Advisor, have you found out any new information?

ADVISOR. Your Majesty, I have consulted with many other doctors, and it has been determined that a spell has been cast on your daughter. It is more powerful than any advice or remedy that is known.

(**PRINCESS** *howls.*)

QUEEN. There, there, dear.

MAIDENS. Don't worry.

(**PRINCESS** *cries and runs off with* **HANDMAIDENS** *trying to comfort her.*)

GRIOT OKOLO. News of the Princess's plight spread throughout the land.

(**BEGGAR CHILDREN** *rise.*)

One day the two beggar children visited the Queen.

BOTH BEGGARS. *(kneeling)* Your Highness.

QUEEN. State your business, quickly.

BEGGAR 1. Your Highness, we dreamed of two birds.

ADVISOR. We have important matters to deal with, hurry up.

BEGGAR 2. The birds dropped seeds as they flew.

BEGGAR 1. And from the seeds grew trees.

BEGGAR 2. And the trees bore both fruit and...

ADVISOR. Shall I send these dreamers away, Your Majesty?

(**QUEEN** *nods yes.*)

BEGGARS. Hair!

QUEEN. What?

BEGGAR 2. Hair! Out of the fruit blossomed the most beautiful hair you have ever seen.

ADVISOR. What kind of babble is this. *(points)* Off with you. You have disturbed....

QUEEN. Wait! Let them finish.

BEGGAR 1. If you will give us food and water for the journey, we will restore your daughter's hair.

QUEEN. What impudence!

ADVISOR. The wisest and most powerful doctors in the kingdom have failed.

QUEEN. Leave before my rage burns you like the summer sun.

ADVISOR. Out, out!

(ADVISOR leads BEGGARS out as QUEEN exits opposite way.)

GRIOT KOUMBA. The children managed to beg a container of water and a small bag of boiled beans and headed toward the place beyond the jungle that they had seen in their dreams.

(BEGGARS re-enter.)

GRIOT ASHAKI. They walked and walked into the night.

GRIOT OKOLO. The distant roar of a lion rumbled through the dark. *(roars)*

BEGGAR 2. *(shivering)* Thank goodness morning is coming. Let's sit and rest and eat a few beans.

(ANTS enter.)

ANT 1. Food. Food. Do I smell food?

ANT 2. I think so. My legs are so wobbldey, woozy from lack of food I don't know if I can locate it.

ANT 1. I'm hibbildy-wibbledy, too. Let's try over here.

ANT 2. Oh, hippo hooves. It's nothing but an empty seed pod. *(sniffing)* Over there! *(more sniffing)*

ANT 1. Oh, rhino rot, there's nothing here either.

ANT 2. But I do smell something. *(sniffs other ANT)* Maybe the sun has singed our antennae and our stomachs are so hungry they think it's food.

ANT 1. Don't go getting any hyena-brained ideas in your head.

ANT 2. The only thing my head has in it is the same thing my feet have.

ANT 1. What is that?

ANT 2. Dust.

ANT 1. I still smell something. Over here. Over here.

ANT 2. You're right. I smell it too.

ANT 1. Look! Beans!

ANT 2. Could you spare us a crumb?

ANT 1. The drought has left us starving.

BEGGAR 1. We know what hunger feels like.

BEGGAR 2. Here. Eat your fill. *(gives them some beans)*

ANT 1. Look how many!

ANT 2. How many?

ANT 1. More than a zebra has stripes.

ANT 2. Yipes!

ANT 1. You are most kind.

ANT 2. Thank you.

    (They scurry off as the **FLOWER** *enters.)*

GRIOT KOUMBA. As the beggar children lifted their water to take a drink, a voice interrupted.

FLOWER. *(gasping)* Excuse me.

BEGGARS. What was that?

FLOWER. Please…. Could you spare me a drop. I am dying of thirst.

BEGGAR 1. A flower!

BEGGAR 2. How did you manage to survive the drought?

FLOWER. I have long roots but they are almost dead.

GRIOT ASHAKI. The beggar children looked and saw that there were only a few sips of water left.

    (**BEGGARS** *look at each other and nod.)*

GRIOT OKOLO. Without thinking of their own needs, they poured the precious water on the flower.

BOTH BEGGARS. Here. *(pours water)*

GRIOT KOUMBA. Color returned to the flower as her stem straightened and her petals unfurled.

FLOWER. Ahhhh. Thank you. You have generous hearts. Thank you.

BEGGAR 1. You are welcome.

BEGGAR 2. We must keep beauty alive in the world.

GRIOT ASHAKI. Refreshed by the water, the flower stretched her bloom toward the sun.

(**FLOWER** *starts off.*)

FLOWER. Good-bye, and thank you.

BOTH BEGGARS. Be well.

(**FLOWER** *is gone.*)

GRIOT OKOLO. Tired, hungry, and now parched with thirst, the beggar children didn't know how they would be able to continue their journey.

GRIOT KOUMBA. As they pondered their dilemma, a bedraggled mouse appeared looking lost and drooping with fatigue.

(**MOUSE** *staggers on.*)

BEGGAR 1. Little Mouse. You look lost.

BEGGAR 2. What's the matter?

MOUSE. I was up on the mountain searching for food with my family and we got separated. Please, could you help me find them?

GRIOT ASHAKI. The beggar children immediately forgot about their own needs.

BEGGAR 1. (*sees* **MOUSE** *looking tired and desperate*) Yes, of course we will help.

BEGGAR 2. Perhaps the object of our own search lies somewhere on the mountain.

GRIOT OKOLO. And so, with the little mouse following, the beggar children led the way up the perilous path that wound along the steep mountainside.

GRIOT KOUMBA. They climbed and climbed and at last came to a wondrous sight.

GRIOT ASHAKI. There, up in the clouds, was a lovely clearing, and in this green oasis, were the two birds from their dream welcoming them to food and drink.

(**MOUSE** *slips away unnoticed.*)

BIRD 1. Eat.

BIRD 2. Drink.

BIRDS. Be our guest.

BEGGAR 1. Mmm…thank you.

(They eat vigorously then suddenly remember:)
Wait, we forgot about the mouse.

*(They look around and realize the **MOUSE** is gone.)*

BEGGAR 2. *(calls out)* Mouse, mouse! It was right behind us, but now it's gone. *(starts to leave to find the **MOUSE**)*

BIRD 1. The mouse has not gone.

BEGGAR 1. Where is it then?

BIRD 2. It is right here

*(gestures as the **MOUSE** appears, followed by the **ANTS** and the **FLOWER**)*

BEGGAR 2. Look, and here are the ants and the beautiful flower.

BIRD 1. We sent them to you.

BIRD 2. It was a test to see if you were worthy.

BEGGAR 1. Worthy of what?

BIRD 1. Worthy of the gift we are about to give to you.

BIRD 2. You may be beggars, but your hearts lack for nothing. You are kind and generous.

BIRD 1. Here is your gift. A seed for a "tree that grows hair," like the one you saw in your dreams.

BIRD 2. Plant the seed in the haughty Princess's garden and each night give it water.

BIRD 1. If you tend it well, you will be rewarded beyond your happiest dreams.

BEGGAR 2. Thank you for this gift.

BEGGAR 1. We will tend it carefully.

BIRD 2. Farewell, and continue to spread your generosity throughout the kingdom.

ANIMALS. *(waving)* Farewell!

BEGGARS. *(waving as they leave.)* Thank you!

(**ANIMALS** *and* **BIRDS** *exit as* **CHILDREN** *walk.*)

GRIOT OKOLO. When the beggars returned, they slipped into the garden of the Princess and planted the seed of the tree that grows hair.

GRIOT KOUMBA. Every night they crept back to water it.

BEGGAR 2. Oh look. A tiny green shoot.

GRIOT KOUMBA. The Princess, who now wore a scarf over her head to cover her shame, was looking at the moon when she saw the beggar children enter the garden and kneel to water the tiny tree.

(**BEGGARS** *leave as* **PRINCESS** *enters opposite.*)

GRIOT ASHAKI. Later that night, she came out to her garden to see what was going on.

PRINCESS. Amazing. Though the land is dry as dust, here is a small tree, green and growing.

GRIOT OKOLO. She was so enamored by the healthy little tree that she added some precious water of her own.

(**PRINCESS** *pours water from her pitcher and exits back to chambers.*)

(**BEGGARS** *re-enter.*)

GRIOT KOUMBA. When the beggars returned the next night, they were amazed.

BEGGAR 1. (**BEGGARS** *stoop to water tree.*) What? Someone has already watered the tree.

BEGGAR 2. Tomorrow let's watch and see who it is.

(**BEGGARS** *withdraw to side.* **PRINCESS** *enters with* **MAIDENS.**)

PRINCESS. Here little tree. Have some water. When all around is dry and withered, how beautiful you are. You shall be my only friend, for you have no eyes to see my shame.

BEGGAR 1. *(coming forward)* You, too shall be beautiful, Princess.

PRINCESS. Who are you?

> (*Wind howls by and blows the* **PRINCESS**'s *scarf off. She screams.*)

BEGGAR 2. Your hair!

PRINCESS. My hair!

HANDMAIDEN 1. It has returned!

HANDMAIDEN 2. More beautiful than ever!

BEGGAR 1. Just as the birds promised.

PRINCESS. I don't understand.

BEGGAR 2. You see it started with a dream.

GRIOT ASHAKI. All through the night the beggar children told the Princess about their dream and their journey up the mountain.

GRIOT OKOLO. When they finished, the sun was rising, and where the little tree had been, a big beautiful tree now stood surrounded by birds.

> (**BIRDS** *fly on chirping.*)

PRINCESS. I'll give them some of my soft hair for their nests. (*to* **HANDMAIDENS**) Give me a cutting blade.

HANDMAIDEN 1. Yes Your Highness.

HANDMAIDEN 2. (*removing a small knife from basket*) Here it is.

PRINCESS. (*offering her hair*) Cut enough for every nest.

HANDMAIDEN 1. That will be quite a bit.

PRINCESS. No matter.

HANDMAIDEN 2. Your hair will not be nearly as thick.

PRINCESS. I have plenty to share. Besides it will grow back.

> (**HANDMAIDENS** *line bird nests.*)

HANDMAIDEN 1. There, all the nests are soft as silk inside.

BEGGARS. What's happening?

HANDMAIDEN 2. The sky is turning black.

> (**QUEEN** *and* **ADVISOR** *enter.*)

QUEEN. Black clouds everywhere.

ADVISOR. It is an omen.

PRINCESS. Did you feel that?

HANDMAIDEN 1. What?

BEGGAR 1. I felt it too.

ADVISOR. It's raining!

ALL. It's raining!

QUEEN. Children, we treated you like beggars, but you have proven to be of noble blood. You shall come to the palace and serve as honored counselors in all things. Let us celebrate the coming of the rains.

ALL. Yes. Let us celebrate.

GRIOT KOUMBA. They all returned to the palace where they were joined by the birds and animals from the mountain.

GRIOT ASHAKI. Together they celebrated the beggar children's spirit of generosity and giving.

GRIOT OKOLO. The children and the Princess lived to a wise old age and always gave care to the trees and birds, and to all living creatures. *(They do so.)*

ALL GRIOTS. Go well, and peace be with you.

(All dance into curtain call.)

(curtain)

GLOSSARY OF ASHANTI WORDS

Griot – (*GREE-oh*) A storyteller.
Koumba – (*Kow-OOM-ba*)
Ashaki – (*Ah-SHOCK-ee*)
Okolo – (*Aw-KOH-low*)
Futi – (*FOO-tee*)
Wo ho te sen – (*woe-HO-tah-sen*) Greetings.